RONALD KIDD

# DREAM BENDER



ALBERT WHITMAN & COMPANY
CHICAGO, ILLINOIS

Library of Congress Cataloging-in-Publication
data is on file with the publisher.


Published in 2016 by Albert Whitman & Company
ISBN 978-0-8075-1725-3


Printed in the United States of America
10 9 8 7 6 5 4 3 2 1 BP 24 23 22 21 20 19 18 17 16

Design by Jordan Kost


For more information about Albert Whitman & Company,
visit our web site at www.albertwhitman.com.

To Yvonne, the dreamer,
and Maggie, the dream

# PROLOGUE

You don't know me. You don't see me. But I am there. Watching. Helping. Bending your dreams.

I watch many. But you are the one I am drawn to. I like the way you sing. I like the way you laugh. I like the way you know what people are feeling.

Do you know what I am feeling? It is fear. Fear that you will change. Fear that you will lose the thing that makes you special. Fear that it will be taken from you.

Fear that I will take it.

# PART ONE

# THE DREAMER

# 1

## CALLIE

I'm a computer.

They say that many years ago, before the Warming, computing was done by machines. Lots of things were. Machines counted and washed clothes and traveled about the City. Some people say the machines talked to each other, but I wonder if that's true. It sounds strange, don't you think?

Computers are people like me. My name is Callie Crawford, and I'm thirteen years old.

My parents tell me I'm pretty, but I'm not so sure. I have blond hair that shines red in the sunlight. My eyes are green. When I smile, I mean it. If that's pretty, then maybe I am.

I work with numbers. I put them together and

take them apart. I juggle them in my head and write them in the stacks of books we keep. The City is a big place, so we need many computers. Our work is important. But sometimes I want more.

Do you ever wonder what's beyond? Beyond the City, with its tall buildings and narrow, twisting lanes. Beyond the land of Between, the wild place outside the City. Beyond the numbers that fill my head. Beyond the everyday things that fence me in and press me down. I think there may be something out there. I want to see it. I long for it, but I don't even know what it is.

Sometimes I catch a glimpse of it, like a flash on the horizon, like a rainbow dipping out of sight. Sometimes I hear it. It sounds like music or the silence after the music stops. I look. I listen. I edge forward, eager to touch it. I can't reach it, but someday maybe I will.

I love the old stories. My father tells them sometimes as we walk to work. Stories are his job. He's a keeper, which means he watches over memories of the past. His specialty is studying myths, stories that have been handed down from grandparents to parents to children, on and on over the years and through the generations.

"His name was Moses," said my father one spring day as we headed to work.

It was one of my favorite stories. My father grinned when he told it, not because the story was funny but because it made him feel good. He is a big man with a kind face and gentle hands. His hair is the color of copper, and his cheeks are dotted with freckles. He has an easy, relaxed way of walking. I walk the same way, or at least that's what my mother tells me.

She's also a keeper. Her specialty is studying old books and documents from before the Warming. She wasn't with us, because she works in a different part of the City. Each morning the three of us make breakfast and eat together, then go our separate ways. My mother was probably already at work, poring over documents that people had found in sealed chests, the upper floors of buildings, the tops of trees, and other places where water didn't reach during the Warming.

"Moses was born in the time of the Warming," my father went on, "when the days were hot and the seas were rising. Water was starting to cover the land, so Moses built a boat and prepared it to live on."

"Did Moses take his family?" I asked. I knew the answer but wanted to hear him say it.

"Of course he did," said my father. "He wouldn't have left them behind. He also took animals—always in pairs, male and female—and people who could do things: builders, planters, keepers, computers. The seas rose, and soon the land was gone. The boat was like a world, with everything the people needed. Babies were born. Moses watched over it all. He was wise and good, a leader of the people."

A group of walkers crossed in front of us, carrying a banner. *Freedom Day*, it said. *Celebrate on the Square!* The walkers filled the street, shouting and waving the banner. I started to push past them, but my father stopped me.

"Walkers go first," he said. "They let you compute. You let them walk."

I watched them go by. The walkers were always moving. Sometimes they held signs; sometimes they delivered messages; sometimes they carried water from the streams to the cisterns so we could use it for drinking and washing. Sometimes they just walked, their feet blistered, their legs strong and thin. Their shouts faded into the distance, and we started moving again.

"Years passed," my father continued. "Generations came and went. Then one day the people found land. One man got off to see if it was safe. He climbed a high peak and looked around. He saw a place with empty buildings and narrow roads."

"The City," I said.

My father nodded. "The people rejoiced. The animals scattered. The years on the boat were over. The City became their new home, and they lived happily ever after."

"How do you know they were happy?" I asked.

He shrugged. "They had each other. They had their work and their memories. What else did they need?"

Many things, I thought. A future to go with the past. A glimpse of what's beyond.

We made our way past the old buildings of the City. There aren't many new buildings, partly because they're hard to build and partly because we like old things. Old things are familiar and reassuring. They're comfortable. You can depend on them.

We study old things—stories, books, objects. We treasure them and learn from them.

My father said, "Remember Mr. Gonzales? Your mother works with him. He studies old buildings. What he tells her is fascinating." My father pointed to a rundown structure of brick and concrete. "For instance, that one was called a bowling alley. He found some heavy balls inside but isn't sure what they were used for."

We passed a building that towered overhead, reaching to the clouds. "That's a scraper," said my father. "People actually lived and worked all the way at the top."

"How did they get up there?" I asked.

"Machines."

It was just one word, but it told me everything I needed to know. Since the Warming, machines haven't been allowed. We aren't supposed to talk about them. I wondered what kind of machine could take you up into the air, but I didn't ask.

Machines aren't the only subject we avoid. There are others: war, violence, art, music.

Some topics are fenced off, dangerous, too hot to touch. I wonder why. Is it really so bad to talk about them? What are we afraid of?

My father and I came to an iron gate. He stopped and gazed inside. Of all the places in the City, this was the most important. It was the cemetery. When I was young, my mother had explained what made it so special.

"It's where people go when they leave the present and join the past. They become part of history, the most precious thing we have."

At the time I didn't know any better, so I asked, "Why is history so precious?"

She smiled. "It tells us where we've been and what we've done. It's why your father and I are keepers. He says a City without history is like a person without memories. How terrible would that be?"

I joined my father at the cemetery gate and looked inside. "Are Grandma and Grandpa in there?"

He nodded. "And Great-Gran and Papa and on and on over a hundred years, back to the time of the ship. I'll be in there someday. So will you."

He took my hand. I shivered. "I like it better out here."

We turned and moved on toward the computing center. One of the few new buildings in the City, it was shaped like a giant box. There was no sign on it because everyone knew what it was. It was the City's brain. Some people thought it was a boring place, but I didn't. Numbers are many things, but they are not boring. They help me think. They form patterns in my head. I am good at making the patterns. But there are some questions that numbers cannot answer.

"Why am I a computer?" I asked.

"That's easy," he said. "You're good at it."

"What if I don't like it?"

My father glanced at me, surprised. "You don't?"

"Not just me. I mean anybody. What if you don't like your job?"

He said, "You stick with it. You learn to like it."

"That doesn't seem right."

"Callie, you know how it works. You go to school, and they watch to see what you're good at. When you're twelve, the choosers pick a job for you—keeper, catcher, computer. It's for the good of the group."

He studied my face. I must have been frowning.

"You're a smart girl," he said. "What if people could turn down jobs and do whatever they wanted?"

"Mom says it used to be that way—you know, before the Warming."

"That's right, and look where it got them."

As we approached the computing center, there was a noise in the street behind us.

Someone cried out, halfway between a yell and a scream. We whirled around and saw a young man racing down the street on a strange, two-wheeled machine.

"What is that?" I asked my father.

He stared at the machine for a moment, then recognition lit up his face.

"I saw a picture once in an old book," he said. "I think they call it a…sickle."

The young man wobbled as he rode, weaving through the crowds, pushing the sickle with his feet. People jumped aside, staring after him. As they did, a group of catchers appeared. Their job was to patrol the streets and make sure people obeyed the laws. People who didn't were taken for counseling, to help them understand and improve. Some people couldn't, and they would be kept in a safe place where they wouldn't harm others.

The catchers closed in. The young man dug in

his heels and tried to stop, but the sickle veered to one side and toppled over. The catchers were on him instantly, pulling him to his feet and grabbing the sickle.

One minute he was struggling with the catchers; the next, they had whisked him away. The crowds drifted off, and I turned to my father.

"He wasn't hurting anyone," I said.

"You know the rules," my father replied. "No machines."

"I wonder where he got it."

My father looked around nervously. "It doesn't matter," he said, draping his arm around my shoulders. "They'll put it away someplace where people won't be getting ideas."

He kissed the top of my head. "Time to work. See you tonight."

He left me at the computing center and moved off toward his office, a little cottage several blocks away. I turned and went inside.

That night, I dreamed again. I was beside a lake, singing. The music danced and swooped, filling the air and lighting me up from the inside. I was glowing, brighter and brighter. I was on fire. Then something moved in and snuffed out the light, like fingers on a flame.

The dream was gone. The music was silent. I was alone in the darkness.

# 2

## JEREMY

"I have a question."

Dorothy sighed. "Again?"

"Why do people dream?" I asked.

"I already answered that one," she said.

"It wasn't a good answer."

Leif Caldwell poked me in the ribs.

"Ow! Well, it wasn't."

I'm Jeremy Finn. Some people say I'm a troublemaker. I prefer to think of myself as an inquisitive genius. I ask questions because that's the way I learn.

Who are we? Where did we come from? Where are we going and why? I keep asking questions, but no one wants to answer.

I'm a dreambender. My job is to poke around in

your head, check out your dreams, and adjust them if needed. You know that dream you were having? Let's tweak it here, twist it there, give it a left turn or a double-inverted flip. Let's bend it until you cry for mercy—but you won't, because you don't even know I'm doing it.

Of course, I haven't done anything yet because I'm still in training. There are five of us, sitting cross-legged in the Meadow under a starry sky. Dreambenders sleep during the day and come out at night when the City people go to bed and their dreams come alive.

Dorothy was our trainer and guide. People said she was so good that she could bend dreams before they started, before the dreamer had fallen asleep. Frankly, I had my doubts. To me, she seemed like your typical middle-aged teacher—stodgy, boring, gray hair in a bun, you know the type. She pursed her lips and gazed at me. Maybe she thought if she stared hard enough, I would go away.

"You may not like it, Jeremy," she said, "but the truth is that we don't know why people dream. It could be a way of resting or playing. It could be a mechanism for sorting our thoughts at night. Maybe it's like taking out the garbage. Whatever it is, we know that dreams can influence what people think and feel and, therefore, what they do."

"Shape a dream, shape a life, shape a world," said Leif.

He was a tall, handsome kid with just one flaw: he was perfect. He was also my friend, if it's possible to like someone who makes you look bad just by walking through the door. His blond hair and big shoulders made me feel puny by comparison. I'm short and thin, with black hair and eyes that are always searching the horizon, looking for answers. Leif was looking for answers too, but his were numbers. Leif loved mathematics and the order it represented.

"That's right, Leif," said Dorothy. "Those were the words of Carlton Raines, the first dreambender. You know the story. He grew up in the time when people lived on the ship. As a boy, Raines discovered that he could see people's dreams. He would lie in his bunk at night, and their dreams would come to him, in fragments and then fully formed, playing out on the ceiling of his room.

"After doing it a few years, Raines learned an

amazing thing: he could change the dreams. At first it was little things—the color of a room, the tilt of someone's head. The more he did it, the better he got. Soon he was changing entire story lines."

"Why?" I asked.

"Because he could," she said.

"Is that a good reason?"

"He was young—sixteen at the time. He was experimenting. You've done that, right?"

"Not with people's thoughts," I said.

Dorothy said, "If that was all he ever did, then it wasn't a good reason. But he was no ordinary boy. He began to wonder about his experiments. What are dreams? How do they affect our waking lives? He explored the ship, seeking out dreamers. Once he found them, he tried adjusting their dreams and then watched the results. Little by little, he learned how to influence their behavior."

I looked at the other students. "Does anyone else think this is creepy?"

One of the students shifted uncomfortably. She was Gracie Morales, a short, dark-haired girl who rarely spoke up.

"I guess I do," she said.

*Thank you, Gracie. Maybe I'm not so strange after all.*

Dorothy smiled at her. "I used to think the same thing. But you know what's really creepy? People running wild, doing whatever they want, spoiling the ecosystem and poisoning the planet."

"One life or many?" said Leif. "*The Book of Raines*, chapter four."

Dorothy nodded. "Raines believed we need to work as a group, not as individuals, and he thought dreams might be the key. As he experimented, he began to notice something. Every once in a while, he came across someone whose dreams couldn't be adjusted. He saw these same people in the dreamscape, watching dreams the way he had.

"Can you imagine what a relief that must have been? He wasn't alone! He scanned the dreamscape and found more people like them. It turned out there was a small group, an elite handful of people whose dreams couldn't be changed but who could see the dreams of others."

"The first dreambenders," said Leif.

Dorothy went on. "He showed them how to change dreams. It turned out he was the only one doing it. The technique is simple, but as you'll find out, it's not at all obvious. Luckily it can be taught, and that's what he did.

"As time went on, he noticed something else. A few of the dreambenders had children, and those children all had the gift. Think of what it meant. This amazing ability would be passed on. The group could perpetuate itself, adding new members as they were discovered. Over time, dreambenders could shape the future. It was a staggering thought.

"Led by Raines, the group met secretly over the next few years to decide how to use their powers. They bent dreams away from negativity, toward hope and confidence. They smoothed over conflict and stressed cooperation. They imagined a world without machines or pollution, a clean world that was simple on the surface but rich and complex beneath, a world they could create by adjusting dreams."

Dorothy continued, "They drew up an agreement, and all of them signed it. People think the new order began when the City was discovered, but it really started that day, when Carlton Raines and his friends pledged to create a new world."

She looked around at the fields and forests ringing the Meadow. Darkness covered the area like a warm blanket.

"A few years later, when land was discovered," said Dorothy, "Raines and the dreambenders sent scouts to locate a place where they could live and work—a quiet, protected area away from the City. They found a hidden canyon that opened up into the Meadow, the small but beautiful place where dreambenders have lived ever since. People in the City don't know about the Meadow or what we do here. It's better that way."

The Meadow was my home. I had grown up there. All of us had. It was our bedroom, clubhouse, and playground rolled into one. The adults lived in cottages as singles or couples, while the five of us, like all young dreambenders, had been raised in the children's house, a big dormitory at the center of the Meadow.

Carlton Raines felt that since the future of dreambending—the future of the earth—was in the children's hands, their upbringing shouldn't be left to individual families. We knew who our parents were but had no special connection to them; we were children of the Meadow.

We were raised by caregivers who watched over us and taught us about the world and our special place in it. They took us around the Meadow, showing us what it was like and explaining why we lived there. They told us about the one place in the Meadow where we couldn't go—the dreaming field, where the dreambenders worked. We would go there someday, when we began bending dreams.

One place we could go when we were younger was Looking Hill, at the edge of the Meadow. Leif and I would climb to the top and peer out over the woods, trying to imagine what lay beyond them. Of course, there was nothing. The woods, called the land of Between, were the edge of our known world. The City was out there someplace, but we didn't know where.

The caregivers had changed as we grew older until, at age thirteen, groups of five were assigned a trainer. Ours was Dorothy.

"In ancient times," she went on, "people used to believe in a place called heaven where life was perfect and everyone was happy. I don't know if such a place exists, but if it does, it's probably a lot like the Meadow."

Behind me, Hannah Chee giggled. "The Meadow is boring," she said.

Dorothy smiled. "It's a simple place. And yes, maybe it is a little boring."

Hannah's brother, Phillip, shook his head. "I love the Meadow. It's quiet, so you can hear the dreams."

I said, "I love it too, but why can't we go to the City?"

No one answered. Crickets chirped. Somewhere in the trees, an owl hooted.

Finally Leif spoke up. "I'd like to."

"I've seen it in dreams," said Gracie. "It's crowded and noisy."

Dorothy smiled. "I wondered how long it would take you to ask. Sooner or later, all dreambenders talk about it. We visit the City in dreams; why can't we go there in person?"

"Well," I said, "why can't we?"

"Because the dreamers live there, and we're not allowed to have any contact with them."

"Have you been to the City?" I asked her. Since we weren't allowed to go, I had no idea how to get there.

Dorothy hesitated, then said, "I went there once on a special assignment. When I got back, I was never so happy to see grass."

"Wasn't it exciting?" I asked.

She thought for a moment. "It was like having someone shout at me all day, every day. It never stopped. The buildings leaned over me. They blocked the sky. I could barely breathe. Believe me, the Meadow is better. Dreams are better."

"What was your special assignment?" Leif asked.

"Nothing you need to worry about," said Dorothy.

I knew that Leif, being Leif, would worry about it. I had a feeling I'd hear about it again.

Phillip glanced at the rest of us, then took a deep breath. "Look, history is fine. Stories are good. But all of us know why we're here. We want to bend dreams."

Dorothy studied the group, watching our faces, judging our mood. Then she turned to me.

"All right then. Jeremy, you go first."

"Me?" I asked. "What do I do?"

"Prepare yourself," said Dorothy. "Close your eyes. Quiet your mind. Imagine a lake. A wind blows over it, then a breeze, then nothing at all. The lake is still. The water is clear."

I tried it.

"My lake is more like a puddle," I said. The others laughed.

"Keep trying," said Dorothy.

"I can't."

"Yes, you can."

I tried again. "The puddle is bigger. But it's muddy."

"You're frightened," she said.

"Maybe I like dirt."

"Focus," said Dorothy.

I tried to concentrate. "There's wind."

"Good."

"I can't get it to stop," I said.

"Maybe the wind is your questions," said Dorothy.

"Questions?" I asked. "What questions?" The others laughed again.

Dorothy said, "Jeremy—"

I looked up. The others watched, grinning.

"This is serious," said Dorothy.

"Sorry."

"Do you want to try it?"

"I think so."

Dreambending might be creepy. It made me nervous. But I had to admit, I was curious. I had heard about it my entire life and wanted to find out what it was like.

So I closed my eyes again. I tried to relax. The puddle became a pond, then a lake. The wind may not have stopped, but it slowed down.

"Are you ready?" asked Dorothy.

I took a deep breath. "Yes."

"Now open your eyes," she said. "We're going to the dreaming field."

# 3

## JEREMY

They say there are a few special places in the world where energy surges and ideas flow, where colors are more intense, where the air is thick and your senses come alive. The dreaming field was one of those places, or so I'd been told. I'd never been allowed there. None of us had. It was where the dreambenders worked.

Dorothy led us there now. We rounded a group of trees, and there it was, stretched out in front of us. We could easily see the other side and could have walked across in just a few minutes. The only building was a large canopy at the back of the field where dreambenders worked in bad weather.

There was dark-green grass, and flowers were

planted in neat groups. Ringing the field was a stand of evergreens. Above it, stars blazed across the sky.

Shimmering under the stars, glowing like ghosts, were the dreambenders. They were scattered over the field—standing, sitting, reclining. Sometimes I forgot how small the group was. There were just a few hundred of us, compared with many thousands in the City. Dreambenders did their work in shifts, rotating through the dreaming field to give each other time off. That night, there were about sixty.

Most of the dreambenders had jobs to keep the Meadow going. In the early evening, before night came, they did these jobs in and around the little cluster of buildings at the eating hall. Planters harvested a modest field of crops. Herders ran a dairy farm, producing milk and cheese. Bakers made bread and pretzels, my favorite. Weavers created clothes. Whatever their jobs, dreams were their calling and their passion. Compared with dreams, everything else seemed pale and inconsequential.

Phillip gazed at the dreambenders and murmured, "They're amazing."

"They look pretty normal to me," said Hannah.

Thank goodness for Hannah. She gave Dorothy someone else to glare at.

"Of course they do," said Dorothy. "You've known them your whole lives. But they're special, and you'll be too. Each one of them contains a world. It's invisible to you, but they can see it. They're in it right now, observing and adjusting."

Soon I would be one of them. The thought frightened me. What if I couldn't do the job? What if I messed things up and ruined someone's life? Worse, what if I *could* do the job? What gave me the right to change a dream? How would I know I was helping?

Dorothy led us to an empty place on one side of the field. She gestured for the group to sit in a circle with me in the middle, then sat down beside me.

"Can someone else go first?" I asked. "What about Leif?"

"Shut up," he said.

Dorothy smiled. She said in a low, soothing voice, "Close your eyes, Jeremy. We'll start with an easy one. I'm scanning the dreamscape, looking for a dream that's simple and clear."

Trying to relax, I scanned it too. So did my friends in the circle. I could feel them with me in the dreamscape. You might say I could see them, though my eyes were closed. We could sense one another's presence.

All of us had roamed the dreamscape since we were little. We did it without thinking, the way other children hummed or clapped or skipped. Dreams flashed by like cards in a deck.

"Ah, yes, here's one," said Dorothy. "The streets of the City are speeding by. Do you see it?"

I looked for motion and saw a blur of people and buildings. "I think so."

"Remember, this is from the dreamer's point of view. We're watching through his eyes."

The dreamer was a young man. I couldn't see him, but I knew. We always did. I'm not sure how.

"He's excited," I said.

It was something all of us had learned from a lifetime of watching dreams. You didn't just get the sights and sounds. You got the feelings.

I said, "How is he going so fast? No one can run like that."

"Good, Jeremy. This is where your questions will help. Can you figure it out? Look down. What do you see?"

"A metal bar," I said. "His hands are gripping the ends. The bar is attached to something underneath, something that's spinning around." I strained to see it. "It's a wheel! He's on a machine."

"Excellent. It's called a bicycle."

"Machines are illegal," I said.

"It's a dream," said Dorothy. "But the dreamer knows what a bicycle looks like and how it feels. Maybe he rode one when he was awake. Maybe he's planning to ride one again. We don't know. But it can't be good. We need to discourage him, so we bend the dream. Are you ready?"

I said, "Riding the bicycle looks like fun."

The words popped into my head and out of my mouth. They do that sometimes. When it happens, my friends shake their heads. *Think before you talk*, they say. I'd like to. I really would.

To my surprise, Dorothy chuckled. "Yes, it does. But machines hurt the group. They're against the rules. So we bend."

"Will this stop him from riding?"

"We don't know," she said. "We're not changing his actions—only he can do that. We're adjusting his dreams. That's all. We'll take a few of his impulses and snip them out, tie them off. Maybe the next time he sees a bicycle, if he can find one, he'll look at it and wonder why he ever thought it would be fun."

"Isn't that mind control?" I asked.

"It's more subtle than that. We adjust people's desires and goals, not their thoughts. Sometimes it works and sometimes it doesn't. Over the years, little by little, through the work of the dreambenders, the world changes. It shifts gradually, like the colors in a sunset. Red becomes pink. Orange turns to rust, blue to indigo. Violence decreases. Order improves. The ecosystem grows stronger. Before you know it, the sun sets and trouble fades away."

"I like the sun," said Hannah.

My eyes opened. I stared at Hannah; we all did. Dreambenders love the night. That's when people in the City sleep, but we're wide-awake. In sunlight, you think you can see everything in perfect detail, but it's an illusion. There's a whole world that's invisible until darkness falls and the stars come out, a world of shadows and wishes, a world of want, of need. People think they live in the sunlight, but darkness is where they truly come alive. At least, that's what we believe.

But Hannah liked the sun.

"It's all right," said Dorothy. She didn't seem concerned, but there was a look in her eyes as she watched Hannah. Trainers usually didn't take notes during sessions, but we knew they were watching us and evaluating. Hannah's comment had registered. Perhaps later Dorothy would write a note in a file.

Dorothy turned to me. "All right, Jeremy. Close your eyes again. Find the dream."

I flipped back to it as if I'd placed a bookmark. The others looked on. We saw the dreamer race through the streets of the City. People gaped, then leaped out of the way.

I said, "How do I bend it?"

It was what all of us wanted to know. Like the people Raines had discovered so many years before—our ancestors—we could see dreams but had never changed them. From an early age we had been told that changing dreams was forbidden to all but the dreambenders. Secretly, though, all of us had tried it. What kid wouldn't? But none of us had succeeded.

"Remember a few minutes ago?" said Dorothy. "The lake? The breeze? Imagine them again."

"I'll lose the dream."

"That's the surprising thing," she said. "The dream stays. In fact, if you do it right, the dream slows down. You can pause it, examine it, adjust it. But first you have to slow yourself down. That's what Carlton Raines discovered one day when he was exploring dreams. He had stumbled on an ancient religion called Booda, involving stillness and concentration, and that day he decided to try it while watching dreams. It turned out that the two practices fit together perfectly, as if they were made for each other, as we believe they were."

"What happened?" I asked.

"Picture the lake. You'll find out."

I tried it.

"I can't," I said. "The dream is in the way. It's distracting me."

"Now you know why children can't do this," said Dorothy. "It's counterintuitive. You want to rush toward the dream and embrace it. But to bend a dream, you do exactly the opposite. Sit back. Be still. Focus."

I tried again. "I can see the lake. It's deeper than before. The water's clear."

"Good, Jeremy. Hold that image in your mind. Now, look up."

Buildings sped by. People stared. Beneath me, the wheels of the bicycle whirred.

"I see the dream," I said.

"Slow it down."

"How?"

"With your mind," she said.

I'm not sure how to describe what happened next. I placed my mind over the dream, the way a fisherman might throw a net. I pulled it close. As I did, the bicycle slowed. The buildings no longer flashed by in a blur. They floated with every detail clear, more slowly with each moment. Finally they stopped. I heard myself breathing.

"Now, reach out," said Dorothy. "Touch it."

I did. To my surprise, I didn't feel the wheels or metal bar. I felt strands, cords, threads, woven together like one of the ancient, faded tapestries in the Memory Museum.

I said, "It's like cloth or a rug. The surface is rough. There are patterns."

"Excellent. Now, find the strand where the bicycle is. See it?"

"Yes."

"Pull it," she said.

"You mean—"

"Give it a yank. Don't be shy."

"What if he stops dreaming?" I asked.

"He won't," she said.

I located the bicycle strand, feeling it with my fingers. I tugged, and it came loose. I held it in my hands like a rope.

Dorothy said, "You're doing wonderfully. Now for the most important part. Tie off the strand."

"Huh?"

"Take the strand and tie it in a knot."

"This is crazy," I said. "It's a dream, not a pair of shoelaces."

"We're working at a deep, symbolic level," she said. "The lake, the dirt, the wind—those aren't real. Neither are the patterns or strands. We don't know much about the mind, Jeremy. We observe it. We use it. We're grateful for it. But we don't pretend to understand. Carlton Raines stumbled onto the technique you're trying."

"If I tie off the strand, will the dream go away?" I asked.

"The bicycle will."

"That's sad. Riding it was fun."

"It was dangerous."

I sighed. In the silence, my breath sounded like the wind. I took the strand and looped it around itself, forming a knot and pulling it tight.

"Congratulations," said Dorothy. "You've bent your first dream."

There was a distant noise, and I realized it was applause. Opening my eyes, I looked around the group. They were smiling and clapping. They had seen me working in the dreamscape, and now they were watching me in a new way. I was someone different and apart, someone unknown.

"That's all for today," said Dorothy. As the others drifted off, she touched my shoulder.

"Are you all right?"

"I feel bad about the dream," I told her. "Maybe it was dangerous, but it didn't seem harmful. It was fun! Now he'll never see it again."

"That's right," she said, "but you will."

"I don't get it."

She gazed at me with a strange look on her face. "Before we bend dreams, we're a part of them.

We gain experience that the dreamers are denied. We like to think that the experience helps us, that it makes us wiser and better able to guide others. But no one really knows. The dreams live on in our minds, unbent, with all their danger and beauty. The dreamers don't have them, but we do. It's the dirty little secret of dreambending."

"Doesn't it bother you?" I asked.

"Sometimes."

She said it almost defiantly. Maybe Dorothy was more than just a lady with her hair in a bun.

"You shouldn't have picked me first," I said. "I ask too many questions."

She said, "I chose you on purpose. You have the seeds of greatness, Jeremy. All of us sense it. You're bright. You're quick. Yes, your questions can get you in trouble, but they can also help you. They could help all of us. It's been years since Carlton Raines started dreambending. Maybe it's time for some new ideas."

I stared out across the field where dreambenders worked in the starlight, looking for danger and snuffing it out, making the world a better place. Then I got up and walked across the grass toward home.

Later that night, I dreamed I was riding a bicycle. The wind blew through my hair. I came to the lake I had seen earlier. The water was deep and still. On the other side, far away, was a sound. It was forbidden. I should have turned away. But it was beautiful.

Someone was singing.

# 4

## CALLIE

This is how computing is done.

You sit at a desk with piles of paper in front of you. The papers are filled with numbers.

Some days you simply add, subtract, multiply, and divide—food costs, mileages, weights, salaries, taxes, water usage, all the hundreds and thousands and millions of calculations that keep the world going. Other days you work on a higher level, observing the totals, arranging them on a page, looking for patterns and meaning. Which neighborhoods consume the most food? Does this affect their buying levels? How do salaries and taxes figure in, and what's the relationship among these factors? The patterns are my specialty. City officials come to me for information. Once I even met the governors.

The patterns are fascinating. Some are beautiful, but they only go so far. I wonder what's beyond the calculations, behind the patterns, over and above and beneath it all. Some days I think I can glimpse it. Other days, all I see are numbers. I find what I can, then make some marks in a book. A collector takes the book. I move on to the next pile.

There are rows and rows of desks in the computing center. My desk is near the door. That way, when the bell sounds for breaks, it's easy to go outside and watch the people. I take deep breaths and try to clear away the numbers that hang around my head like cobwebs.

On break the next day, I looked out over the busy street and remembered the young man on the sickle. He had worn an expression I didn't often see in the City. His face had shown fear, but there was also excitement. He wasn't thinking about the past. He was entering the future. It couldn't be counted or predicted. Anything could happen. He might crash. He might fall. He might go so fast that he would lift off the ground and fly between buildings, over the scrapers, up to the sun and stars.

I saw three girls my age painting the wall of a storefront next door. They had white coveralls that were splashed with color. What I noticed most was the way they talked and laughed. They seemed to be friends, which was unusual in the City. Most of us were too busy to have friends. We had families and jobs and responsibilities, but not many friends, and certainly not much time to laugh. I watched them for a while, then wandered over.

"I like your clothes," I said.

One of the girls, small and wiry, looked up. "They're kind of messy."

"That's what I like," I said. "You know—the colors. The mess."

She glanced at one of her friends, a pudgy girl with a blond ponytail, and rolled her eyes.

I wasn't supposed to see it. The third girl, dark and lanky, chuckled.

"They think you're strange," she told me. "I think that's good."

She held out a paint-stained hand, and I shook it. She had a firm grip. "I'm Eleesha."

"Callie," I said.

"The eye-rollers are Juanita and Pam. We're

painters. In our spare time, we're painters."

I cocked my head. "Huh?"

Eleesha glanced around to see if anyone was watching, then opened her bag. Inside were some small wooden frames with canvas stretched across them. The canvases were blank except for one, on which was painted a picture of the City—people, animals, buildings. The picture throbbed with color, as alive as the scene around me.

"Did you do that?" I asked.

Eleesha nodded. "We work on these after dark, using leftover paints from the daytime. I did this one a few nights ago."

"Don't show her that," said Juanita, scanning the area.

"She's okay," said Eleesha. "I can tell."

"Why are you worried?" I asked Juanita. "It's just a picture."

Juanita and Pam exchanged glances. Juanita said, "We use the City's paints. They might not like that."

"You know how they are," added Pam.

"Who do you mean by 'they'?" I asked.

"You know," said Juanita. "The people in charge."

"The governors?"

I thought about the elected board that ensured the City ran smoothly. We called them governors. But I had a feeling Juanita and Pam were referring to something else.

"Let's not talk about it," said Pam nervously.

"Why shouldn't we?" asked Juanita. She turned to me, her eyes flashing. "Do you ever have the feeling we're not in control? I'm not talking about laws or rules. I'm talking about...something else. Something you can't see."

Eleesha said, "Sometimes when I wake up in the night, it seems like someone is in the room with me. Then I look around, and no one's there. Does that ever happen to you?"

I thought about it for a minute. "Maybe. I thought it was just a dream."

Juanita said, "Whatever it is, we gave it a name. Them."

"You probably think we're crazy," said Pam, giggling anxiously.

"It's just a game we play," said Eleesha. "It's our secret, okay?"

"Sure," I said.

Eleesha studied my face. "You seem different."

"From what?"

She nodded toward the computing center. "From the other people who work there. They look at us like we're dirty. But this is just paint. We're doing our jobs, the same as they are."

I took another look at the little canvas in her bag. "Your picture is beautiful. You can almost see the people moving."

Eleesha glanced at her friends then seemed to make a decision. "Would you like to come?"

Juanita glared at her, but Eleesha barely noticed. She watched me, her gaze connecting us as surely as a thick, strong cable.

"Come?" I said. "Where?"

"To the Midway. We'll be painting tonight. It's better after dark. We bring lanterns. You'll see."

"I don't know..."

"You can watch us," she said. "You can try it yourself if you want."

The bell sounded at the computing center. It was time to work.

"Tonight?" said Eleesha. "Come late, after everyone is asleep."

She scribbled directions on a scrap of paper and

handed it to me; then the three of them turned and went back to their job.

Watching them, I wondered what it would be like to roam the City in the middle of the night. The thought thrilled and frightened me. There might be danger. There might be beauty.

Maybe I would be surprised. Maybe, like the sickle rider, I would fly over the buildings and up to the stars.

* * *

The Midway was a jungle of shapes and shadows. There were rusted-out machines, but no one knew what they were for. One was tall and round, like a giant wheel. Another had rails that had sprung free, sticking out like a bad haircut. Metal carts littered the area, apparently made to sit in, though I couldn't imagine why.

The Midway was in the City but somehow not a part of it. It was as if, when people had reclaimed the City, they had taken one look at the Midway and given up. There were rumors it had been devoted entirely to fun, if you can imagine that.

The place had been fenced off years ago, but according to the directions Eleesha had given me, there was a way in. I found it at the end of an alley, where some of the fencing was loose. I squeezed inside, wondering why I was there.

Getting there had been surprisingly easy. I had waited until my parents were asleep, then opened my window and climbed out. Catchers patrolled the streets, but there weren't many of them. City dwellers love sunshine and fear darkness. We have lanterns to use at night, but most of us prefer the daylight, so we go to sleep and wake up with the sun.

I hurried along, pausing every once in a while to look at the stars. Soon the Midway loomed in front of me, its strange shapes silhouetted against the sky. A few minutes later, I was inside.

"You made it!" said a voice.

I glanced up and saw Eleesha holding a lantern. She was wearing the same paint-splattered coveralls as before, and her face had a warm glow. I hadn't noticed before, but there was something sad about her.

"My friends didn't think you'd come," she said. "Then we heard noises, and I knew it was you."

I shrugged. "I'm not sure why I came. Just curious, I guess."

She led me around the giant wheel to a series

of curved steps leading down to an open area. The steps seemed like places where people would sit to watch a show. I wondered what kind of show might have been given before the Warming. I pictured the people sitting there, laughing and applauding, delighted by something I couldn't imagine.

Juanita and Pam were sprawled halfway down the steps, lanterns at their sides, with paints and the canvases spread out in front of them. Juanita looked up when we approached.

"Oh great," she said.

"Don't let me interrupt you," I told her.

"You already did."

I looked over her shoulder at the canvas she'd been working on. It was full of dark colors—maroons, purples, blacks. At the center was a bright red slash. At first I thought the canvas had been ripped, then I realized it had been done with paints.

I nodded toward the canvas. "What is it?"

She shrugged and looked away.

Next to her, Pam seemed completely absorbed in her painting. Eleesha noticed me watching her.

"Pam goes deep," she said. "Sometimes it takes her a while to come back out."

Pam's canvas couldn't have been more different from Juanita's. Yellows leaped out, with bright blues and greens. Something was taking shape, but I couldn't tell what.

I looked up at Eleesha. "What are you painting?"

"Nothing yet," she said. "I'm waiting for an idea to float by."

"Is that how it works?" I asked.

"Sometimes. Other times it comes so fast, you can't keep up."

Juanita, who had gone back to her canvas, said, "Can we just paint?"

"Sorry," I said. "I'll watch."

I settled on one of the steps. Eleesha set down the lantern and went back to her canvas.

I'm not sure how long they worked. They had been talkative in the City, but now they were silent and thoughtful. Words didn't seem necessary. Color was everything.

A boxy brown structure took shape on Eleesha's canvas. I recognized it as one of the mysterious carts that dotted the Midway. Juanita's slash darkened, and she added smaller slashes.

Out of Pam's bright colors, an odd-looking

building emerged. As she finished the picture, she shook her head as if coming out of a trance. Seeing me, she smiled.

"Oh, hello. We saw you in the City."

"I like your painting," I told her.

"It's the Music Place."

*Music.* The word made my skin tingle. If you said it out loud, people flinched and changed the subject. The funny thing was, I liked saying it. I liked thinking about it. I always had, though I wasn't sure why.

I studied Pam's canvas. It showed a building with points and curves, like a stack of shapes, like the sails of a ship.

Eleesha set down her brush and reached inside her bag, bringing out a container and four cups. I wondered why there were four, then realized she must have been hoping I'd come.

"Let's have some tea," she said.

She poured it from the container into the cups and handed them out. We sat on the steps, sipping quietly.

"I like this," I said. "Not just the tea—all of it."

"We don't do it just because we like it," said Juanita. "We need it. We look at the world and see things. We put them down on paper to show how we feel. We're painters—not the City kind. Our kind. My kind."

As she spoke, I felt something stir inside me. I turned to Pam. "Eleesha said you go deep. What does that mean?"

Pam's cheeks reddened. "I'm not sure. Things seem different when I paint."

Eleesha said, "Have you ever had the feeling you were doing what you were made for?"

She nodded toward a moth that fluttered around her lantern. "Moths seek light. Birds fly. Spiders make webs. What about people? What about you? What were you made for?"

"I'm a computer," I said.

Juanita snorted. "See? I told you."

Eleesha said, "The choosers tell us what we are. Maybe they're wrong. They want the three of us to paint buildings, but we paint pictures."

"They don't like art," said Pam. "I can't imagine why. It's beautiful."

"It's more than that," said Juanita. "It's *ours*, not something chosen for us. *We* choose. All of us are choosers, or should be."

Eleesha nodded. "The funny thing is, sometimes we forget."

"Forget?" I said.

"The pictures. The art. The feeling of the painting. Isn't it strange? We forget the things we love the most."

An idea flickered in the darkness, then disappeared. I tried to get it back, but it was gone.

"Luckily," said Eleesha, smiling at her friends, "it doesn't happen for all of us at the same time. I forget, and they remind me. They forget, and I remind them. The next night, we're back at the Midway, painting."

Juanita eyed me uneasily. "Don't tell anyone. You have to promise."

"You can trust me," I told her.

"That's what they said too."

"Who?" I asked.

"Some people. We thought they were friends. We showed them our paintings, and they told the catchers. Ever since, we've had to be careful."

Juanita studied the red slash on her painting. "Nobody understands. The keepers are the worst. What's so special about old things? Why should we worship cemeteries? I'd rather make new things, like our paintings."

I thought of my parents. Did they understand? Were they stuck in the past? I decided not to mention them, for now at least.

When we finished our tea, Eleesha and her friends packed their things. A few minutes later we split up and headed home. I started toward my house but wasn't ready for the night to end. Turning back, I looked for Eleesha and saw her duck down a side street.

I hurried after her, hoping to catch up. I started to call out, but something about the way she moved made me hesitate. She darted from shadow to shadow as if she didn't want to be seen.

At the far end of the street, she looked around nervously, then slipped past a gleaming metal gate. Beyond it were trees, bushes, and grass, like a park but different. Perfectly maintained, lovingly cared for, it was the last place I would have expected to find Eleesha or her friends. It was a cemetery.

# 5

## CALLIE

I followed, afraid to speak but too curious to turn back. When Eleesha entered the cemetery, her steps slowed and her shoulders slumped. She paused to pick a handful of daisies, then moved along a row of gravestones, sure of where she was going but apparently not eager to get there.

At the end of the row, in front of a small granite monument, she stopped for a few moments. Then she continued on to a bench under a nearby tree. She cleared away a bouquet of withered flowers from the bench, replaced it with the handful of daisies, and sat down.

Watching from behind a tree, I felt terrible. I didn't like sneaking around or spying on people. My mother always says, "When you're wrong, admit it. Face up to your mistakes." So I took a deep breath and stepped into the open.

"Hello again," I said.

Eleesha flinched and looked up. "You followed me." There was pain on her face, and her eyes were wet.

I said, "I'm sorry. I wanted to talk some more and was surprised to see you come here."

Eleesha glanced around, taking in the perfect rows of gravestones but looking somewhere past them. "My friends don't know about it. They hate this place. They say it's where people worship the past."

I had discovered Eleesha's secret. It seemed only fair to tell her mine.

"My parents study the past," I said. "They're keepers. I should have told you before."

She took it in, nodding. I had the feeling you could tell Eleesha anything and she would do the same thing: listen, nod, try to understand.

"I'll leave," I said, turning to go.

"Don't you want to know?" she asked.

"Know what?"

"Why I'm here."

I said, "Only if you want to tell me."

She inclined her head toward the gravestone where she had stopped. "My grandmother's buried over there. I used to visit her grave when I was little. It was so peaceful. But that's not why I come back now."

I wanted to know but decided to let Eleesha tell me in her own way.

She said, "If a twin dies, are you still twins?"

I remembered something my father had once told me. I said to Eleesha, "When you lose an arm, you can still feel it. It could be the same with twins."

"Maybe," she replied.

"Did you have a twin?"

She nodded. "We weren't identical. He was a boy. We didn't even look that much alike. But there was something special between us."

"What happened to him?" I asked. "Unless you'd rather not say."

"I want to. My parents don't like to talk about it, and it makes Pam and Juanita uncomfortable."

I sat on the bench next to her. We were quiet for a while. When I'd been to cemeteries before, they had seemed clean and formal. I had never realized how lovely they could be.

"Two years ago," she said, "the strangest thing happened—strange and awful. One night I heard my brother screaming and moaning like he was having a terrible dream. I went in to check on him and found him sweating and writhing in bed. I tried to hold him down, to help him or to comfort him. Finally, after a long time, he went back to sleep. I stayed with him, sitting by his bed. I guess I fell asleep. When I woke up, the bed was empty.

"We searched the house and the neighborhood. We told the catchers. We talked to his friends. We put up signs. Nothing.

"We searched for weeks and finally gave up. We discovered a few other cases like it, where people had had bad dreams, then disappeared. Maybe they'd run away. Maybe they had been hurt and couldn't get help. Maybe there had been foul play. None of them ever came back."

I wondered how hard it would be to lose a brother, especially a twin.

"The funny thing," said Eleesha, "was that all the people who disappeared were about my brother's age. He was twelve."

"Why would that be? I don't understand."

"I don't either," she said.

Eleesha stroked the bench tenderly and gazed off into the distance. "For the longest time I didn't believe he was gone. We'd had that special connection, and I didn't want to let go. Deep down, I knew that if he were still alive, he would have contacted me. But there was nothing. Not a trace.

"I wanted a place where I could go to remember him, and I thought of my grandmother's grave. This bench was close by. I come here to talk to him. Every few days I bring fresh flowers. I miss him."

Eleesha picked up a daisy and sniffed it. Her words explained the sadness I had noticed in her face. They also explained her eagerness to have me join the group. Eleesha had friends, but somehow, deep down inside, she was lonely.

There were footsteps behind us and the light from another lantern. We looked up and saw a catcher.

"What are you girls doing here?" he asked.

He was an older man with a stern gaze. I'd seen him on patrol near the computing center.

"Visiting my grandmother's grave," said Eleesha.

"It's late," said the catcher. "You should be at home, sleeping."

I said, "We were just talking. We're not causing any trouble."

"This isn't the place to talk," he said. "Or the time."

He studied me. "I know you. Your father's a keeper. Did you tell him you're here?"

"Not exactly."

He reached down, took my arm, and pulled me to my feet. "All right, get up, both of you. Let's go."

"Where?" asked Eleesha.

"Home," said the catcher. "I'll let you go this time. But don't let me catch you out at night again."

Eleesha hung back. I guess she wanted to say good-bye—to me or maybe to her brother.

"Go!" the catcher told her.

She caught my eye, then reluctantly moved off. When she was gone, the catcher walked me to the gate. Outside, he let go of my arm.

"Are you going to tell my father?" I asked.

He surprised me by smiling. "When I was your age, I used to sneak out at night. It seemed exciting. I explored the city. Maybe even a few cemeteries."

"What happened?" I asked.

"I grew up," he said. "Now, go home. Go to bed."

"Thank you."

I turned to leave.

"Oh, and one other thing," he added. "Stay away from that girl."

"Eleesha?"

"I've seen her by the computing center. She and her friends don't follow the rules."

"She seems nice."

"She's trouble," he said.

# 6

## JEREMY

Colors were everywhere. The girl reached out and swirled them like finger paints. They formed mountains and tunnels, bridges and roads. She swirled them again. They were dogs and cats. There was a horse. She climbed onto its back and rode into the night.

"This dream is nice," I said.

"I agree," said Dorothy. "Pass or stay?"

"Pass."

"Yes," she said.

"That was hard. I wanted to stay."

"I know," she said.

The man was in a rickety old house. Bats hung from the ceiling. Bugs skittered across the floor.

I said, "This is disgusting."

"Focus, Jeremy," said Dorothy.

There were halls, endless halls. With every turn the man found himself in another hall that stretched into the distance and out of sight.

"He's troubled," I said, "but the feeling is vague. Maybe there's a problem, or maybe he's just worried."

"Pass or stay?" asked Dorothy.

"There's not enough to go on," I said. "Pass."

"Good," said Dorothy.

The little boy was behind bars. He gripped the bars and shook them. They held firm. He tried to squeeze between them and get out. It was no use.

"He's in jail," I said. "Maybe I should help."

"Watch closely," said Dorothy.

The boy jumped up and down. The ground was soft. But it wasn't the ground. It was a blanket.

I said, "Hey, that's not a jail. It's a crib."

Dorothy chuckled. "Good. You let the dream play out. You didn't jump to conclusions."

"Pass," I said.

A woman sat in a kitchen, drinking coffee. There was a fluttering sound, and a blackbird landed in the open window. The bird let out an awful shriek, and anger rose up inside her. She lunged toward the window and splashed her coffee on the bird. It kept shrieking. She looked around, saw a knife, and grabbed it.

"Uh-oh," I said. "This one, right?"

"Yes," said Dorothy.

I pulled the strand and tied it. The knife folded in on itself and disappeared. Instead of a knife, the woman picked up a loaf of bread and tore off a piece. She offered it to the bird. The bird plucked it from her hand, then flew off across the sky.

I said, "She wanted to kill it."

"Now she doesn't," said Dorothy.

"Is she dangerous?" I asked.

"In real life? Probably not. We all have violent impulses. But now there's one less. We change the world an impulse at a time."

"It's flat," I said.

"Pardon me?"

"The world we're making—it's flat and dull. Less interesting."

"Maybe so," said Dorothy, "but it's better than the alternative."

They were called little dreams, the kind that flicker in the dark, shine briefly, and disappear. Most of our dreams are little dreams, and those were the ones Dorothy had been helping us with, the way she was helping me that night.

The five of us were spread across a corner of the dreaming field, alone together, each exploring a different part of the dreamscape. Leif sat up straight as usual, an intense expression on his face. Gracie fidgeted, trying to get comfortable. Hannah smiled. Phillip lay back on the grass, gazing into space.

During our weeks of training, we had learned that the dreamscape shifts constantly and, like the sky, is different every night. Some nights they are clear and sparkling. Some are foggy. Sometimes the wind kicks up, scattering debris. Sometimes clouds move in and dreams darken.

Lightning flashes, thunder rolls. Across the dreamscape, in a thousand ways on a thousand nights, people suffer, tremble, cheer, throw back their heads and laugh.

Each dream is different. Some are simple, and some are complex. It's part of what keeps us coming back. The differences call for judgment, and ultimately that's what dreambending is about.

What goes? What stays? What gets tied off and removed? Trim, adjust, move on. Mistakes are made—they always are—but if we do our jobs, the big picture will be fine. The world will turn to the better, slowly, gradually, imperfectly. One degree at a time.

That's what Dorothy told us. I told Dorothy it didn't seem right. Just because we had the power didn't mean we should use it. But I had to admit that I liked it.

Dorothy moved from person to person, checking our work, suggesting, encouraging.

These days I barely saw her gray hair or bun. What I saw were her eyes. They seemed to take in everything, not just outside but inside too.

As we had explored the dreamscape over the past few weeks, I had learned why training didn't begin until we were thirteen. Dreams could be brutal. They could be violent and grim.

There was love and there was sex, and the two weren't always the same. We had glimpsed these things as children, but our minds had flinched and turned aside, the way you might shield your eyes from a bright light. Now, as dreambenders, we couldn't look away. It was our job to observe and decide.

Some couldn't do it. Dorothy told us stories about people who were overwhelmed by the dreamscape. Some became addicted and couldn't bring themselves to leave. Others got lost and weren't able to find their way out. A few tried to do damage. They hid out among the impulses, creating fear and revulsion. Eventually, of course, all of them were caught by the watchers, the group that observed and managed the dreamscape, and they were given other jobs. They stayed in the Meadow, part of a small group who didn't bend dreams but were still able to help and be a part of the community.

All except one.

That's what people said anyway. They told stories about a dreambender who had wandered off into the dreamscape and over the hills. One day he was in the dreaming field, and the next he was gone.

No one, not even the watchers, could discover where he went or why. But he was out there, they said, roaming the dreamscape, haunting dreams. They called him Boogey. Personally I doubted the story, but some people believed it. Hannah did. So did Phillip. For some reason Boogey scared Leif to death. More than once I had found Leif cowering in his bed, shaking uncontrollably, convinced that Boogey was after him.

"You're doing fine," Dorothy told me. "Good work with the blackbird."

She started to move off toward the others. Watching her, I thought about what I'd seen and heard in the dreamscape.

"I have a question," I said.

She turned back to me, smiling. "What a surprise."

"We bend dreams about violence and machines and pollution. I get that. But what about music?"

Dorothy blinked. "What about it?"

"Those other dreams are dangerous. Music isn't, but we bend it anyway. Why?"

I'd wanted to ask that question for a long time, but no one wanted to hear it. Music was something we weren't supposed to talk about. My friends and I did, of course, but we always whispered. The word seemed mysterious, loaded, ready to explode. But the thing itself, the melody that had come floating to me in the night, was beautiful.

Dorothy's smile faded, and she gazed into the distance. "I wondered when you'd get around to that. Lots of us wonder about music. Few have the courage to ask. I was one of them."

"What did they tell you?"

"They fidgeted and didn't say a thing. So I asked around. Finally, I spoke to a caregiver at the children's house and saw a flicker of something in his eyes. He pulled me aside and checked to make sure no one was listening."

"And?"

Dorothy looked around, the way the caregiver must have done that day. She turned back to me. "I wouldn't tell most people, but I think you should know. The caregiver I spoke to that day had heard stories about the time when the ship landed and the City was rebuilt. He said the founders were determined to prevent another Warming."

"So they banned machines," I said. "Everybody knows that."

"They believed machines had caused the Warming, but there was something else. They thought the people had become distracted, focused on themselves instead of the world, on feelings instead of facts."

"Feelings?"

She sighed. "Art. Dance. Especially music. They said because of music, people fiddled while Rome burned."

"Huh?"

"It's an old expression. No one knows where it came from. It means being distracted during a crisis. When the Warming came, the leaders tried to shut down the concert halls, but the musicians wouldn't let them. In the daytime, the musicians helped fight off the crisis like everybody else, but at night they gave concerts. They kept making music, claiming it was important. Even though times were difficult, music gave life meaning. It gave people hope.

"The founders disagreed. Years later, when the City was settled, they didn't just ban machines. They banned music—not through laws but by spreading the word that music is evil, something you don't talk about and don't do."

I said, "Do you really believe that?"

Dorothy gazed at me. "Part of me does. The world works better when people focus on their jobs."

I snorted. "That world is boring. Music is beautiful."

When Dorothy answered, I got the sense she was

arguing with herself as much as with me. "Maybe music is beautiful. But we can't have everything we want, Jeremy. As a dreambender, you should know that. We make trade-offs every day. We snip things out. We prune the weeds so plants can grow."

"Music isn't a weed," I said. "It's a plant, maybe an important one."

"Some people would disagree with you—Carlton Raines, for one."

"Carlton Raines was scared," I said. "So were the founders. They knew you can't control music. You can't fence it in. It's pure feeling. Is that so bad?"

"Maybe it is if your job is to manage the world. It's a delicate balance. Music is dangerous. So we forbid it to protect all of us."

She squeezed my shoulder, then moved off toward Gracie. I went back to the dreamscape, where I erased an impulse to steal, a craving for chocolate, and a fascination with violence.

Of course, all I really changed were the dreams, not the people, but the dreams were where they lived. Their wishes, hopes, and fondest desires were there, and I was with them. I rounded the edges and softened the colors. I flattened the world. Meanwhile, in my own mind, the original dreams lived on, with the colors bright, the feelings raw, the melodies strange and lovely.

# 7

## JEREMY

They came in boats.

Running through the Meadow was a river, and in the river was an island. On special nights, boats cast off from the island at sunset, moving across the orange water like dragonflies. The color stretched over the river and up the sky in a continuous band. Blue and purple waves rippled, spreading in patterns through the world, the way dreams do.

They were the watchers. When we saw them set out across the river, we stopped and stared.

"Why are there twenty-four of them?" I asked Dorothy. "Why not twenty-three or twenty-five?"

Leif snickered. "Do the math. Eight boats, three to a boat. It's all the room they have."

It was a joke, but it was also typical of Leif—using math to find the answers.

"They tried different numbers," Dorothy said. "Twenty-four worked best. Enough to manage the dreamscape but not too many."

"How can anyone manage the dreamscape?" asked Gracie. "It's so complicated."

"That's why little dreams are handled by the dreambenders," said Dorothy. "It leaves the watchers to manage big dreams."

"All my dreams are big," said Hannah.

"Your mouth is big," said Phillip.

Dorothy looked out over the river. The watchers were halfway across, rowing with slow, steady strokes.

"You've all seen big dreams," she said. "You've bumped up against them. They're the ones we stay away from."

"The nutcases," said Hannah.

Dorothy's eyes flashed.

"Sorry," Hannah mumbled.

Leif said, "Above all, respect for the dreamer."

It was from *The Book of Raines*. Had he memorized the whole thing?

"Big dreams are recurring dreams," said Dorothy. "They don't flicker and die out like little dreams.

They come back again and again, carving a channel in the mind. The channel gets deeper each time. These are the dreams that can change lives. Some involve mental illness, as Hannah suggested. Some are obsessions. Some show intense longing."

"What if the longing is for something good?" I asked.

"Sometimes it is," said Dorothy. "Sometimes it isn't."

"Who decides?"

Dorothy studied me. "The watchers decide. It's part of the job."

"And what if they're wrong?" I asked.

"They're usually right."

The boats reached land, and the watchers got out. They wore robes to distinguish them from the other dreambenders. The robes were white and billowed in the breeze. The watchers fanned out across the dreaming field. Every so often, one of them would stop next to a dreambender, and the two of them would talk in low voices.

"What are they doing?" asked Gracie.

"Giving assignments," said Dorothy.

"For the Plan," said Leif.

The Plan. I'd heard that term my whole life, but

whenever I had asked about it, my caregivers would tell me, "You'll see. Wait until training." They had said it so often that the Plan had started to seem like a fantasy, like Boogey or the Tooth Fairy.

"Leif is right," said Dorothy. "The Plan is real. You've wondered what the watchers do on that island? They work on the Plan. The original Plan, called the Document, was drawn up by Carlton Raines and the founders. It was made up of long-term goals. Over the years, the watchers have adjusted those long-term goals to fit new developments, but the underlying purpose is always the same: to keep the people safe."

"That's it? The watchers adjust a few goals?" said Hannah. "It doesn't sound like much work." Leif shot her a look, and she shrugged. "Well, it doesn't."

Dorothy smiled. "It's a good question. Watchers don't just work on the Document. Keeping those long-term goals in mind, they roam the dreamscape, looking for big dreams that can cause trouble. The watchers discuss what they've found, and based on those discussions, they draw up a list of dreams to be bent—risky dreams, dangerous dreams, dreams that could hurt someone. Then they decide which dreambender should handle each one. Every day they write up a report called the Plan. When it's ready each evening, they come to the Meadow and make assignments."

"Have you worked on the Plan?" I asked.

"All of us have," she said. "Periodically we rotate and become watchers. I had my chance two years ago."

"Could we try it?" asked Phillip.

"Be patient," Dorothy replied. "You'll get your turn someday."

One of the watchers approached us. He was a tall man with dark skin and close-cropped hair. He wore the same flowing robe as the others, and it flapped behind him like a pair of white wings. He went to Dorothy and said something we couldn't hear. Surprised, she glanced at him, then turned to me.

"Jeremy," she said. "Arthur wants to talk with you."

Great, I thought. Now what had I done?

Arthur studied me, then came over and put his arm around my shoulders. "Let's walk," he said.

He led me to a corner of the Meadow, away from the others, where he sat on a rock and motioned for me to join him.

"Am I in trouble?" I asked.

"Dorothy tells me you're gifted," he said.

"She does? I wasn't even sure she liked me."

"Dorothy is an old friend. I can tell you she's hardest on those who show the most promise."

I tried to hold his gaze. "I have to warn you. I ask a lot of questions."

He watched me. "Well?"

"Huh?"

"Ask away."

I was nervous but also curious. In the end, curiosity won out.

"What's it like on the island? Why do you go there? How do you pick big dreams? What happens if you don't? What happens if you do? What gives you the right? And why do you want to talk to me?"

Arthur laughed.

"What's so funny?" I asked.

"I like your style," he said.

"Are you going to answer my questions?"

He looked off into the distance, as if trying to remember something. "All of us have questions. Maybe not as many as you, but we all have them. We've learned that it's best for people to answer their own."

"I can't. That's why I asked you."

He said, "The answers will come, I promise."

"Then why are we talking? What good will it do?"

I got up from the rock. He reached out and gripped my arm.

"Jeremy, you show great promise. Most dreambenders are good at little dreams. A few are skilled at big dreams. Every once in a while, a dreambender comes along who has other skills, different skills. Someone who wants to know more. More can be good. Of course, more can also be dangerous. So we watch that person carefully."

"Are you watching me?"

"Oh yes," he said.

"And?"

"We think it's time for the next step. Follow me, Jeremy. There's a big dream I'd like to show you."

* * *

A man was considering suicide. He stood on top of a cliff, gazing down at a pile of broken rocks.

"Does he have the dream often?" I asked Arthur.

"Every night. Lately it's been more intense. The cliff is higher. The rocks are more jagged."

"He's scared," I said.

"Anything else?"

"There's something strange," I said. "When he considers jumping, he seems almost...happy."

"That's the bad part," said Arthur. "And the part that we can use."

"How?"

"You'll find that it works best if we don't make new thoughts. We use what's already there. Think about the dream. How can we use the man's happiness?"

I looked down at the rocks, then up at the sky. Clouds billowed. A hawk circled overhead. It gave me an idea.

"Can I try something?" I asked. "You might think it's strange."

"Go ahead."

I reached out to touch the dream, the way Dorothy had taught us.

"Hey, this feels different," I said. "The surface is rougher. The strands are thick, like cables."

"Big dreams are hard," said Arthur. "They're tough."

I found the strand containing the hawk and pulled. It wouldn't budge. I tried again. It took all my strength, but finally I managed to work the strand free and loop it back toward the man. I could feel his thoughts slide away from the rocks and up to the sky. With a surge of excitement, he jumped off the cliff.

Next to me, Arthur stiffened. "Jeremy—"

But the man wasn't falling. He floated. He dove. He swooped over the rocks. Catching an updraft, he shot past the cliff and into the clouds. His arms were spread wide, but they were no longer arms. They were wings. He was a hawk.

"My goodness," said Arthur.

"Pretty good, huh?"

"Indeed," he said. "An elegant solution."

"Do you think he'll jump? In real life, I mean."

"Maybe," said Arthur, "but it won't be because of the dream."

"Will the dream come back?" I asked.

"Probably. But he'll be flying, not jumping, at least for a while. The watchers will check on him. We may need to bend the dream again. But now we know how."

"Can I do another one?" I asked.

"Let's stop for tonight," he said. "Don't worry though. I'll be back."

He was true to his word. Over the next several weeks, whenever the watchers arrived, Arthur would come to me. I had to admit, it made me feel good.

I built up to two and then three big dreams a night. Every once in a while, another dreambender would wander by in the dreamscape. When they sensed a big dream, they would move to avoid it, as we had been taught to do. In the same way, I avoided big dreams that Arthur had not assigned to me.

One night though, a big dream seemed especially intense. It gave off a dark-green fog that rolled across the dreamscape, and I couldn't resist looking. As I approached, an awful scream rang out, and the dream suddenly went dark. There was confusion, then silence. The dream was gone.

I asked Arthur about it the next time I saw him. Looking off into the distance, he seemed to pick his words carefully.

"You know, Jeremy, bending big dreams is a serious business. It doesn't always work out the way we'd like it to."

"I know. It's hard."

"Yes, it is," said Arthur. That's all he would say.

On the nights between Arthur's visits, I worked on little dreams with Dorothy and my friends. Ever since my conversation with Dorothy, I'd been noticing how often the dreams involved music—sometimes a song, sometimes just the feeling of a song. It was always there, bubbling beneath the surface, and our job was to keep it down.

I also noticed that since Arthur's arrival, my friends had treated me differently. Leif didn't shove me the way he used to. Hannah wouldn't make fun of me. Phillip was the worst.

Whenever I looked around, he was holding a door for me or offering to run errands. "I don't have errands," I told him. "I'm thirteen years old."

"Right, right, of course," he would say. Then he'd do it again.

On Arthur's first few visits, he worked next to me, but then he saw that I could bend the dreams without his help. He said I had a knack for it. After that, he did what the other watchers did, stopping by to give me assignments and then moving on.

I liked working by myself. I felt strong and useful. I was a dreambender—not a kid fooling around, but a worker with an important job. I was part of the Plan. I was improving the world and keeping it safe.

Wasn't I?

## PART TWO

# THE DREAM

# 8

## JEREMY

Leif seemed to be perfect, but he could surprise you. In fact, that was one of his favorite things. He would slip away, then pop out at you. That day was no different.

"Boo!" he said, leaping out from behind a bush.

I jumped, the way I always did.

"Got you that time," he said, grinning.

It happened so often that I'd taught myself a rule: never forget about Leif. If you did, you'd be sorry.

He chuckled softly to himself, and we moved on. We were walking along the river, headed for the dreaming field. It was the time of day I liked best. The sun was getting low in the sky. The colors were softening. The air had cooled down, and a breeze blew gently across the water.

"Hey," I said, "do you remember when we used to sneak off in the mornings and go swimming?"

"We should have been sleeping," said Leif. "Even dreambenders have to dream."

"Yeah, I know. *The Book of Raines*, chapter blah-blah-blah. Is that all you ever think about?"

"It's important," he said.

"Can't we just relax once in a while? You know, laugh together? Be friends, like the old days?"

He smiled. "You ask too many questions."

Months had passed since Arthur had first come to me. Dorothy's lessons had ended. Our training was over. Now the group spent its nights bending dreams. Most of the dreams were little, but occasionally, when the watchers came, they would tap someone on the shoulder and assign a big dream. I was the only one in our group who always got selected and always by Arthur. I liked it when he told me I was special. Mostly, I liked the dreams.

Leif liked the rules. He always had. It was one of the reasons he was good at math. When he wasn't quoting *The Book of Raines*, he was asking about the fixers, the people who enforced the rules. For a while I think he was jealous that Arthur had picked me, but then he began following the fixers. He offered to help. They took him up on it, and his path was set. He was still part of our group, but we saw less of him.

Suddenly, one day, when the fixers arrived in the dreaming field, Leif was with them. I asked him about it, but his answer was vague. After that, he was a fixer. We set out together every day, but he went one direction and I went another. Sometimes it bothered me, but then I thought about the way I had been pulled aside. We had both been chosen, just for different things.

We reached a fork in the path. He slapped me on the back. "Be good."

He had been saying that since we were little. It used to be a joke between friends. These days, considering his new job, I wondered if it had a different meaning.

"What if I'm not?" I asked.

He drew a finger across his neck, a grim expression on his face. Then he burst out laughing and trotted off down the path.

* * *

"There's one kind of dream we haven't talked about," said Arthur that evening as we strolled together across the dreaming field. "Of all the big dreams, it's the hardest to bend."

I asked, "Can I try?"

Over the past few months, I had seen lots of big dreams, some woven as tightly as steel mesh, and had bent them all. At first I'd been unsure of myself, but I'd gained confidence quickly. I would scan the dream, spot an entry point, and make an adjustment. It seemed easy to me, though Arthur assured me it wasn't. He said the new type of dream, the kind we hadn't yet talked about, would be even harder.

"These dreams are stubborn," he said. "You can't just change them once and be finished. They keep coming back."

"Why?"

Arthur studied me. "You like asking questions. Let me ask you one. Of all the human emotions, which is the strongest?"

I remembered what I'd been taught in school and what I'd learned from my friends.

"Love?"

"Good," said Arthur. "And after that?"

Hate? Joy? Jealousy? It was hard to say. I decided I liked asking questions more than answering them. I recalled the dreams I'd seen, and a thought occurred to me.

"Hope?" I said.

He eyed me appreciatively. "Dorothy always said you were smart."

"Hope is stubborn," I said. "It keeps coming back."

Arthur nodded. "It's about the future—not what was or what is, but what's going to be. It's a feeling, a wish. How do you change that?"

I thought of my own hopes. I liked to joke around, but I really did have some—to help people, to make the world a better place, to be a dreambender. Every once in a while, I wondered if dreambenders really did help people, but most of the time I believed it was true. I hoped it was true.

"Think about this, Jeremy. Hopes clash. Let's say you hope to be the best dreambender, but I do too. What happens?"

I shrugged. "Someone's going to lose."

"What if my hope doesn't just clash with your hope? What if it clashes with everyone's hopes?"

"Everyone's? Is that possible?"

"What do you think?" asked Arthur.

By then I had gotten to know Arthur pretty well. He knew that the way to catch my interest was by asking questions.

"Are you talking about the Document?" I asked. "That has our long-term goals, right?"

He chuckled. "You're really very good, Jeremy. The Document isn't just about dreams. It's a blueprint for living. It shows what we can be and how to get there. When Carlton Raines and his friends created a world without machines and pollution, a beautiful place where we could all live in peace, they did it by using the Document. We still do, along with the daily Plan."

I tried to follow what he was saying. "The Document helps us shape the world," I said. "And people's hopes don't always fit in. They work against our goals."

"Right."

"So, when that happens, what do we do?"

"I think you know the answer," he said.

Sometimes the truth moves in circles. The conversation was back where it had started.

"Those are the stubborn dreams," I said. "The ones we were talking about."

Arthur nodded. "Maybe I dream of being a war hero. Maybe I want to build machines. My dreams could be courageous, even beautiful, but if they don't fit the long-term goals, we have to bend them. For the good of the group."

"Can I do one?"

"I thought you'd never ask," he said.

* * *

Her mind was quick and lovely. She had a talent for numbers. And she was restless. I could tell that right away.

"She seems unhappy," I said. "Do you know why?"

"Hope," he said. "It's all about hope."

I had found an open spot in the field and settled onto the grass and into the dreamscape. Arthur stood beside me.

"What does she hope for?" I asked.

"Music," he said.

He tried to say it casually but couldn't hide the feeling in his voice. I remembered what Dorothy had told me about music and how we snipped it out like a weed.

Arthur said, "Music is strong in this one. It's distracting her. She has an important job as a computer, and we need her full attention. Work on the distraction, Jeremy. Eliminate the music."

Across the field, a woman called Arthur's name and gestured for him to come. He glanced back at me. "I need to go. You'll be fine, right?"

"Sure. No problem."

He moved off, leaving me alone with the dream.

I sat back and watched, trying to get my bearings. Some people would dive in right away and start changing things. Gracie was like that, maybe because she was nervous. I found that it was better to start slowly, scanning the dream and getting a feel for the dreamer.

She was on a mountain. Somehow it had a hallway and doors, dozens of them. Looking on from behind her eyes, I saw the dreamer open a door. Beyond it was an empty room with a man at one end and a woman at the other. They were reaching out for each other but could never quite touch.

"Mom! Dad!" she called. They didn't hear her.

She pulled the door shut and opened the next. Numbers spilled out like a swarm of ants. They crawled over and around her, moving up her legs and into her eyes and ears. Moaning, she slammed the door. The numbers fell away, piling up at her feet like dead leaves.

She hesitated in front of the next door. I could hear her ragged breathing. She was worried about what was behind the door. Finally, she took a deep breath and pushed it open. She was facing a mirror.

It's funny what happens with dreams. You start by watching from the outside, and before you know it, you're inside and it seems like yours. Then something jolts you, and suddenly you remember you're only a visitor. That's what happened with the mirror. I looked at it, expecting to see my own face. Instead, I was staring at a girl.

She wasn't exactly beautiful. Her nose was a little crooked. Her mouth was full and expressive. Her skin wasn't perfect, but her hair was. On the line between blond and red, it seemed to glimmer back and forth between the two. As I watched, she pushed it behind her ears. She blinked, and I gasped. Her eyes, the color of emeralds, bore into me with an intensity that was frightening.

Without thinking I ducked, then sheepishly

looked back. She studied her reflection, as if she was searching for something and didn't know what. I felt a longing deep inside her.

That's when I heard it. Someone was singing.

It was the voice I had noticed in the dreamscape before. This time, though, it wasn't off in the distance. It was close by, just over the dreamer's shoulder. She turned and moved toward it. Her heart leaped, and I knew this was what she had been searching for.

She hurried past the doors and down the mountain. The path was familiar, worn smooth by footsteps from a hundred dreams. She walked more quickly, then began to run. Something was up ahead, and it filled her with joy. She rounded a turn and came to a lake. Beside it sat the dreamer.

Her features glowed as if she were golden, as if she came from the sun. It hurt to gaze at her, but I couldn't look away. Her head was thrown back, and she was singing. Her voice throbbed and pulsed like a living thing. It jumped. It danced. It filled the sky. It was terrifying, and it was beautiful.

With a feeling of absolute rightness, the dreamer approached the singer and stepped inside. Two became one—dreamer and dream, singer and song.

There was a job to do. I had to stop her from singing and eliminate the music. For the good of the Plan. For the good of the group.

I couldn't do it.

# 9

## CALLIE

I woke up singing.

It was the oddest feeling—new but old, familiar yet utterly strange. I didn't know I was a singer, but I was singing.

My voice was strong. It was beautiful. Where had it been all these years? How could I have held it inside? It was gushing out like water over a dam, and there was no way to stop it. I couldn't. I didn't want to.

I pulled back the covers and sprang out of bed, singing as I went. My room seemed bigger. The details were more vivid. I went to the window and looked out. The City was bustling as usual, but today it made sense, as if there might be a reason for it all.

Someone knocked on the door. "Is that you?" called my father.

I threw it open and gave him a hug. "It's me. It's really me."

He pulled back and stared at me. There was fear in his eyes. "Why were you singing?"

"I don't know," I said, "but I like it."

I took a deep breath and began to sing again. I didn't know what the song was. Maybe it didn't matter.

When I stopped, my father shifted uncomfortably. "Callie, we can't have music. You know that."

"Why not? It makes me feel good."

When he turned away, I went to my closet to get dressed. It contained a few clothes we had bought from the weavers—simple, dark clothes made to work in, not to distract. Reaching to the back of the closet, I pulled out a shirt that was bright yellow, the color of daffodils. My mother had bought it for me one year on my birthday. Almost embarrassed to look at it, she had told me it was for special occasions.

I got dressed and went out to the kitchen, where my mother was putting breakfast on the table. When she saw me, she dropped a plate. It crashed to the floor, scattering eggs and bread.

"That shirt," she said.

I grinned. "Isn't it beautiful?"

I knelt and cleaned up the spill, singing all the while. I sang for the joy of food and the kindness of my mother and the pleasure of being alive. When I finished, I saw my parents huddled together, listening.

"Stop," said my mother. "Please."

"I can't," I said. "I don't want to."

After breakfast, my father walked me to work, and I sang. People crossed the street to avoid me, but I didn't care. My father cringed, and I laughed.

"It's fine," I said. "It's great."

"It's dangerous," he said.

"Why?"

He didn't answer, and I realized it was because he couldn't. He'd been told music was dangerous—all of us had—but no one had said why. The danger was more a feeling than a thought, and I wondered where it came from.

"Just be careful," he told me finally. He kissed me good-bye, and we headed off to our jobs.

Inside the computing center, I sang as I worked. A little while later, the manager came to see me.

"Would you like to talk?" she asked.

"Not really," I said. "It's a beautiful day, isn't it?"

She didn't understand. Who could blame her? After all, she was a computer. And suddenly, in a flash, I knew that I wasn't.

At the break, I went outside and sang. People stared and edged away from me, but I barely noticed. A moment later, I felt a hand on my shoulder and heard a familiar voice.

"Callie?"

It was Eleesha. Behind her were Juanita and Pam.

"I didn't know you were a singer," said Eleesha.

"I didn't either," I said.

Pam gazed at me. "I like your shirt."

Juanita elbowed her.

"Well, I do," said Pam.

Eleesha was watching me. "You seem happy."

"Like we are when we paint," said Pam.

"I am," I said. "Today I'm happy."

Juanita said, "We haven't seen you since that night. Where have you been?"

It was true. I'd been avoiding them, afraid that the catcher would see us again and tell my father. But how could I explain that to Juanita without giving away Eleesha's secret? I saw Eleesha watching me, shifting nervously.

Finally I shrugged. "I get scared when it's dark."

"The darkness is exciting," said Pam. "It's lovely."

Eleesha brightened. "We'll be back at the Midway tonight. Would you like to come? You can sing while we paint."

It sounded wonderful. Suddenly, imagining an evening of color and music, all my worries seemed foolish.

"I'd like that," I told her.

I made dinner that night, the way I always did, except this time I sang. My mother came into the kitchen, concerned.

"Is something wrong?" she asked.

"Why do people keep asking me that?"

She slid over to the counter where I was cutting up the ingredients for a salad. Putting her arm around me, she rested her head on my shoulder.

"Callie, we love you. We want the best for you."

"The singing is fine, Mom. I know it. I can feel it."

After dinner, my father and I washed the dishes. I decided not to sing, because I could see that it was upsetting him. Besides, there would be plenty of time for music later at the Midway.

When the sun set, I kissed my parents good night and headed for my room. I was planning to be up late, so I stretched out on my bed to take a nap before leaving.

I woke up an hour later. The house was dark and silent. I knew my parents were asleep.

I rose and sat on the edge of the bed. I noticed the sleeve of my yellow shirt. The color seemed garish.

I thought of Eleesha and remembered her invitation. I pictured the three girls painting by the light of a lantern and tried to imagine myself sitting beside them, singing. Just a few hours before, it had seemed mysterious and exciting. Now it was null, blank, void—zero, as we say in the computing center.

Singing? Sneaking away? Leaving my warm, cozy bed?

What could I have been thinking?

# 10

## JEREMY

"You did what?"

Arthur's eyes blazed. He gripped my arm. I wouldn't have guessed he was so strong.

"I decided not to bend her dream," I said. "It was so beautiful."

It was the following night, and Arthur had come back to check on me.

"Beautiful?" he said. "Of course it was beautiful. What's that got to do with it?"

"I couldn't bring myself to change it. I thought maybe...I don't know. Maybe the Plan was wrong."

He let go of my arm. "This is my fault. I wasn't strict enough. You were so gifted. I thought you'd understand."

"Understand what?" I asked.

"We don't question the Plan. We do it. That's all."

"It's created by people," I said. "People make mistakes."

Arthur sighed. "It's not a question of mistakes. It's about patterns. The watchers don't just make them up or decide on a whim. We don't flip a coin. The patterns are woven over months and years. Each decision is based on the ones before it, and the next decision on that one."

"But you have a choice, don't you? You could change things."

"Within limits. But not outside the Plan."

"If we never change the pattern, life keeps going straight down the path. Tomorrow is like today. Today is like yesterday. What kind of world is that?"

"A solid one," said Arthur. "A safe one."

"A dull one," I said.

Arthur grunted. "You would have liked the Warming. There was plenty of excitement then."

"Look, Arthur, I let her sing. Is that really so bad?"

"It was music!"

The look in his eyes was the same one I'd seen

in Dorothy's. To me, music was beautiful. To them, it was frightening.

Arthur's shoulders slumped. "We're about to find out how bad it is. You have to appear before the Council."

* * *

If you didn't look closely, it would seem like an ordinary sort of place. It was a little cottage on the island, with green shutters and stone walls. Who would have guessed that, night after night, it was where the watchers decided the fate of the world?

Arthur took me there in one of the boats. It was a trip I had always wanted to make, but not under these circumstances.

"Just tell them the truth," Arthur said as we rowed. "It's all you can do."

We pulled the boat up onto the island and made the short walk to the cottage, where Arthur opened the door and motioned me inside. The place seemed bigger than it did from the outside. We were in a room with windows along two sides. The walls were dotted with lamps, and at one end of the room was a fireplace with flames that fluttered up the chimney but didn't seem to heat the room. In the center was a large, flat table with a few chairs. A big sheet of paper had been spread across the table, and pencils were scattered nearby.

I whispered to Arthur, "Is that—"

He nodded. "The Plan. The one for tonight."

Two watchers, a man and woman, leaned over the table and spoke in low voices. Others circled around, talking among themselves, taking notes on clipboards, occasionally checking with the man and woman. The watchers would nod and write something on their clipboards, then move off past a neatly printed sign on the wall.

> Never meet the dreamer.
> Never harm the dreamer.
> Always follow the Plan.

At the end of the table was another sheet of paper that had been rolled up and tied with string. As we watched, a man came by and picked it up. Carrying it to the fireplace, he opened the screen and set the paper inside, where it smoked, then burst into flame. The other watchers stopped what they were doing and gazed into the fire until the paper had disappeared up the chimney.

"That was last night's Plan," Arthur explained.

"Why did he burn it?" I asked.

"Today is paper. Tomorrow is fire. Yesterday is smoke."

I had heard the expression since I was little. Now I knew where it came from.

"It's a tradition," said Arthur. "It reminds us that we shouldn't dwell on the past."

I had another thought but didn't say it. Burning the Plan kept the work secret. If no one saw it, they couldn't ask questions about it.

After a few minutes, the woman at the table looked up and smiled. "Hello, Arthur." Turning to me, she said, "You must be Jeremy."

"Yes, ma'am."

Arthur had told me to be polite. Dreambenders always were, he said, out of respect for one another and for the job.

"Follow me, please," said the woman.

"Where are we going?" I asked.

"To the Council chamber."

Growing up, my friends and I had learned about the Council. We knew there were three Council members, and they ruled on big issues and problems, one of which apparently was me. The Council met on the island in a special chamber in the cottage.

The woman led us through a door into a smaller room. The walls were paneled in wood. In the middle of the room was a long desk with three chairs behind it and a gavel resting on top. A fourth chair was on the near side, facing the desk. A man and woman sat behind the desk in two of the chairs. Like the watchers, they wore robes, but these were a deep maroon. The third chair was empty, as was the fourth. The woman who had brought us into the room led me to the fourth chair, and I sat down. Arthur stood behind me.

"This is Jeremy Finn," the woman told the others. She bowed slightly, then left.

I waited. Arthur had told me that besides being polite, I had to be patient. It wasn't my best quality.

I leaned over to him. "Is this the Council? How come there are just two of them? Who sits in the third chair?"

He shot me a look. I knew that look: shut up.

A moment later, another door opened and a woman entered wearing a hooded robe. She settled into the empty chair and pushed back the hood to reveal a face I knew well.

"Dorothy!" I said. Covering my mouth, I mumbled, "Oops. Sorry."

"Hello, Jeremy," she said. "I see you're as eager as ever. And you still haven't learned to follow the rules."

"Are you on the Council?"

"She's the chairman," said the man to her left, whose name I learned was Ching-Li. "Some people say she *is* the Council."

Dorothy waved off the remark. "We're all the Council."

"I thought you were just a trainer," I said.

She stared at me. "Jeremy, training is our most important job."

I thought of Leif and the way he liked to quote Carlton Raines. *Shape a dream, shape a life, shape a world.* Apparently they really believed it.

The woman next to Dorothy shifted uncomfortably in her chair. "Can we get started?"

Dorothy straightened up and nodded. "You're right, Louisa. This is a hearing, not a school lesson. Arthur, tell us about the case."

Arthur stepped up beside my chair and described

our work together, mentioning the big dreams I had worked on and the stubborn dream he had brought me.

"There was music," Arthur explained. "I thought he could bend it. He has unusual powers."

At the mention of music, I could see the three of them tense up. Something frightening had entered the room.

"Go on," said Dorothy.

When Arthur told them about the singer's dream, Ching-Li gaped at me.

"You didn't bend it? You let her sing?"

"It was beautiful!" I said.

I stopped, remembering what Arthur had told me. If I argued, the punishment might be worse. And no matter who was in charge or how well I thought I knew her, punishment was what the hearing was about.

"Jeremy was on his own," said Arthur. "As he should have been. As we all are. He made a mistake."

Louisa shook her head. "He ignored the Plan! He defied it."

"He's young," said Arthur. "He shows great potential."

"He always has," said Dorothy, studying me. I

wondered what she saw.

Ching-Li said, "Potential is a sword. It cuts two ways. In the wrong hands it can kill."

"I didn't hurt anyone," I said. I knew I should have kept quiet, but I hadn't done anything wrong, and I certainly wasn't a killer. "I helped her. In the dream, she was happy. You should have seen her."

Dorothy looked up at Arthur. "And how did you respond?" she asked him.

"This evening I discovered what Jeremy had done. When she dreamed again, I made a repair. She'll be fine."

"A repair?" I said. "You bent her dream?"

"Silence!"

It was a voice I had never heard Dorothy use—cold like steel. She spoke as a stranger. "Be grateful, young man. You may not know it, but Arthur saved you. Punishment is based on damage. Arthur repaired yours, so you won't get the ultimate penalty—at least, not this time."

"The ultimate penalty?"

"Banishment from the dreamscape forever."

I tried to imagine it—a life without dreams, except my own. For someone who roamed the dreamscape the way children play in the grass, it was impossible to imagine.

Dorothy said, "We'll be easy on you this time, thanks to Arthur."

"You mean, I can still bend dreams?"

She looked at me as if I'd lost my mind. "Bend dreams? You can't even look at dreams."

Lifting the gavel, she pounded the desk. It sounded like a rifle shot. "You're banned from the dreamscape for one year."

* * *

Afterward, coming back in the boat with Arthur, I gazed at the nighttime sky. Usually I saw dreams there. There were pictures, sounds, feelings—another world. Now that world was closed to me.

"Can I at least visit the dreamscape?" I asked Arthur. "You know, as a guest? I won't change anything."

He stared at me. "Don't you understand? You're banned. If anyone sees you in the dreamscape, the ban won't be for just a year. It'll be for life."

A breeze blew over the water. It was warm, but I shivered.

Arthur dropped me at the dreaming field and

moved off toward the other watchers. He spoke with them, and they glanced in my direction. I wondered what they were thinking. Jeremy Finn, screwup. Jeremy Finn, outlaw. Jeremy Finn, criminal.

I looked across the field. Dreambenders were moving about in this world but living in another one. It would be a long time before I could join them.

Until then, what would I do? What *could* I do? Sit on the grass? Stare into space? When I stared, what would I see?

"Are you okay?"

Turning around, I saw Gracie. Her dark eyes were troubled.

I tried to smile. "I'm fine."

Hannah and Phillip came up behind her. Phillip nodded toward the island. "What happened over there?"

I started to make something up, then stopped. What was the use? One way or another, they would find out. So I told them, starting with the boat ride and ending with the Council's ruling. Usually Hannah would laugh and say something funny. Today she wasn't smiling.

"There was music? You didn't follow the Plan?"

"You should have seen this dream," I said. "You should have heard it."

Phillip shook his head. "I hope it was good."

Over his shoulder, I saw Leif watching us from a distance. I tried to read his expression but couldn't. I wanted to rush over and tell him what had happened. Somehow, though, without knowing how or why, I had a feeling he already knew.

# 11

## JEREMY

I started spending time at the Memory Museum, a small building near the children's house. When we were little, our caregivers had taken us there to see items that had survived from before the Warming: objects made of metal and plastic, things that floated. I especially loved some old tapestries and paintings that, before the Warming, had been sealed in a church for safekeeping. They showed a world long gone, even from our imaginations.

The caregivers had explained that dreambenders respected the past but didn't dwell in it. The important thing for us was the future—envisioning it, planning it, shaping it to be safe for everyone. It was our tapestry, our canvas. And I was shut out of it.

Fascinated by the old objects in the museum, I took up collecting. I searched the Meadow, looking for things the museum keepers might have missed. Collecting was easier in the daytime, so I shifted my schedule. At first, being awake during the day felt uncomfortable, but I got used to it. Most dream-benders were asleep at that time, so I didn't have to deal with their questions and stares. I liked that. But there was something else. I began enjoying the sunshine—not just its warmth, but the way it made things jump out at you, clear and distinct.

One sunny morning, I found three beads hidden in the grass—bright, colorful balls with holes in the middle for stringing. I carried them in my pocket and liked to cradle them in the palm of my hand.

An oddly shaped object made of plastic was wedged beneath a bush. When I pulled it out, I saw that it was a toy vehicle of some kind. There were front and back wheels, a kind of comb jutting out in front, and a connector at the back, as if the vehicle were designed to pull something. Obviously the toy depicted a machine of some kind. I tried to imagine a kid playing with it, but I couldn't. I was careful not to show it to anyone.

I literally stumbled across my best find. I had taken a long walk away from the dreaming field and out to the woods that lined one edge of the Meadow. As I walked, I tripped on something. Part of a rounded metal object was poking up from the ground. I got a stick, dug around it, and finally managed to lift it out of the dirt.

It was the strangest thing, just big enough to hold in my hands. Two metal tubes were fastened together, with glass at each end. The glass in one cylinder was cracked, but the other was fine. I cleaned the glass, and without knowing why, I raised the tubes to my eyes and gazed through them at a nearby tree.

"Hey," I exclaimed. "Hey!"

I had started talking to myself. I guess that's what happens when you spend so much time alone. Most of the time I mumbled, but this was different. I was seeing something truly amazing.

The tree looked tiny and distant. Taking the tubes from my eyes, I checked the tree. It was still just a few yards from me. I looked through the tubes again, checking things—the grass, my feet, a bird. All of them seemed far away.

I turned the tubes around and looked through

the other end. The tree was right on top of me, wonderful in its detail. I could see every ridge in the bark, every leaf on the branches. A worm inched its way across one of the leaves. The worm was green with red spots. It stopped and munched on the edge of the leaf.

"Hello, little guy," I said.

As I studied the worm, I wondered what I'd be able to see when things were far away.

Holding the tubes carefully, I climbed to the top of Looking Hill. Bringing the tubes up to my eyes, I gazed back toward the dreaming field. A mower was working there, keeping the field neat and preparing it for the evening session. He was so close that I seemed to be floating in the air just over his shoulder.

I called and waved. "Hello!" He didn't hear me.

Swinging the tubes sideways, I shifted my view to the river and the island. The cottage was nearby, almost close enough to touch. Smoke drifted from the chimney, all that was left of yesterday's Plan.

When Leif and I used to climb Looking Hill, we had gazed at the forests of Between. I remembered something he had told me one day.

"Between what?" he had said.

"Huh?"

"What do you think it means? If it's Between, there's something on each side, right?"

For some reason that had made me uncomfortable. I said, "I'm the one who's supposed to ask questions."

"Let's say we're on one side. What's on the other?"

"How should I know?"

"Think," he said.

"All I know is the Meadow," I told him. "Plus what I see in dreams."

"And?"

"And what?"

"What do you see in dreams?" he asked.

I shrugged. "The City."

He grinned. I asked him why, but he never told me. Now I thought of it again and wondered what he had meant. Leif always seemed to know things the rest of us didn't. I wasn't sure how he knew, but he did. Maybe he learned things from the fixers he liked to spend time with. It set him apart from the rest of us and gave him a kind of power.

Thinking of Leif's questions, I turned away from

the Meadow and, using the tubes, looked out over the woods toward the empty horizon.

"Something's there," I murmured.

A faint shape appeared, shimmering like a ghost. It was tall and thin, a tower of some kind. As my eyes adjusted, more towers materialized behind it. There was a whole row of them, wispy as webs, the color of the sky. I lowered the tubes. The towers disappeared, leaving the horizon empty once again.

I had seen those towers before, but not from this angle. In fact, they were as familiar as the streets and faces of the dreamscape, because they were part of it. They were always there, a constant backdrop.

I said, "They're in the City! The City's on the other side of Between."

A thought came right behind it.

"I can go there."

As quickly as it came, a question followed.

"Why?"

It was just one word—simple, honest, the question beneath all my questions. I lowered the tubes, and the singer's face floated in front of me. Her eyes sparkled and her hair shone.

What would it be like to see her in person? We

didn't need to have any contact. I wouldn't meet her or speak with her. I just wanted to watch her and know she was real.

But it was more than the singer. I wanted to meet the people whose dreams we bent. I wanted to see the place where they lived—not in the dreamscape but in real life. I wanted to think about why we changed their dreams and what kind of world we were shaping. Going there was against every rule I'd ever learned. If I got caught, my life as a dreambender would be over.

A feeling rose up inside me like a thick, hot liquid. It bubbled up and overflowed, and there was nothing I could do to stop it. It was dangerous. It was stupid. But I had no choice.

"I'm going to the City," I said.

# 12

## JEREMY

To reach the City, I would have to go through the land of Between. It was a strange thought. No one went to Between.

Between was wild. Between was at the edge of the Meadow. My friends and I didn't know much more than that. We had all seen it—trees and vegetation, forming a wall beside the open spaces. In the Meadow we didn't like walls, so we stayed away.

Anyway, if you were a dreambender, why would you want to go there? The waking world, no matter how wild, seemed boring next to the dreamscape. All the excitement was inside your head. You loved the Meadow because it was calm and quiet, the perfect backdrop for dreams. Why venture beyond it?

Why explore? Why take chances? Why ask questions unless you were me?

How big was Between? I thought about that a lot. Finally I decided it must be just wide enough for dreambenders to cross when they had to—two days' walk? Three days? Dorothy must have crossed it once when she made her mysterious trip to the City, and if she had done it, I certainly could.

Being on a different schedule from my friends made it easy for me to slip away. The next morning, after they had returned from the dreaming field and gone to bed, I took the metal tubes, put some food and clothes in a backpack, and set out. I poked around the bushes for a few minutes as if I were collecting. Then, checking to make sure no one was watching, I entered the woods and the land of Between.

It seemed to be a relatively flat area, crowded with trees and a few small streams. There were so many trees, in fact, that it was hard to get a sense of the place. Entering Between was like going inside a room. I was used to open spaces and the sky; suddenly there were walls and a ceiling—tree trunks and branches—and I couldn't see the sun. I had met people who hated small spaces and I had never understood it, but just for a second I knew how they felt.

The trees closed in on me. Thinking of the singer, I shook my head, took a deep breath, and plowed ahead.

I had expected a path, but of course there wasn't one because so few people went there. Progress was slow as I made my way among the trees. I looked up through the branches, checked the position of the sun, and used it to move in the right direction.

Every once in a while, I'd hear a branch rustle or a twig break. I would halt, my heart racing, only to see a squirrel or a bird. Mostly I saw trees. I had never known there were so many of them.

I stopped for lunch and then dinner, if you could call them that. It was cheese and pretzels, the only food I'd been able to grab on my way out of the Meadow. After dinner, when the sun went down, I curled up beneath a tree and slept.

I woke up during the night. For a moment I didn't realize where I was and got scared. Then I saw the stars twinkling between the branches. Dreambenders love stars. They're the canvas we paint on. Somewhere beyond the trees, people were sitting in the dreaming field, looking at those same stars. Somehow that thought made me feel better.

I woke up the next morning and plunged back into Between. I grew to hate the shade. I would gaze up, searching for the sun. It was a moving target. I began to wonder if I had changed direction. Once or twice, I saw things I was sure I'd seen before. But who could tell? It was trees, all trees.

I'd been hoping to use the tubes to find the way, but branches blocked my view. I was in a small, restricted world, where everything in sight was close enough to touch.

I ran out of food the morning of the third day. "Nice going, Jeremy," I said, munching on the last pretzel. "Way to plan ahead."

What if the walk across Between took ten days, or twenty? What if I was going in circles? By that afternoon I was scared. By the evening, fear had given way to hunger. I tried to think about the singer, but I found myself imagining griddle cakes and pumpkin pie.

That night, my dreams of food were interrupted by a noise, and I woke up.

"Who's there?" I called out.

I heard another noise. Panicked, I jumped to my feet and ran. I must have gotten turned around, because when I stopped, I didn't know where I was. My sense of direction was gone, and so was my backpack. The next morning I used the sunlight to look for the pack. By noon I had given up.

That's when I saw it.

It was a footprint—just one. I thought it might be from a dreambender, then noticed that the foot was bare. I found another print, and another, of different sizes. Checking the surrounding area, I stumbled across a cave. There were no people inside, but there was something even better.

"Food!"

I realized I had yelled the word, but I didn't care. The food was separated into several piles: berries, roots, flowers. They weren't the kinds of things I usually ate, but that didn't stop me. I grabbed berries by the handful and stuffed them into my mouth. When those were gone, I tried the roots. I even ate some flowers. The tastes were strange, but they were delicious.

"Hey!" someone yelled.

Before I could turn around, he had jumped on

my back. I tried to throw him off, but he held on tight. I had never been very strong, and without food I was even weaker. After a while I stopped struggling. He slid off my back and pushed me against the cave wall.

He was a boy my age with a dark face made darker by smudges of dirt. He wore ragged clothing and no shoes. His hair stuck out in all directions like the rays of the sun. Beneath it, his eyes gleamed.

"You stole our food!" he said.

"I'm sorry," I mumbled, feeling terrible. "I was hungry."

"Get your own food."

"How?" I asked.

He stared at me. "Gather it. Pick it. Kill it and cook it."

"Kill it?"

"You know—squirrels, rabbits."

"You eat rabbits?" I tried to imagine it.

He studied my face and clothes. "Who are you?"

"Jeremy."

"You don't live here."

"I live…at the edge of the woods." I pointed in the direction I'd come from. "That way."

Then I pointed in the opposite direction. "No, that way." I shrugged. "I might be lost."

"Are you from the City?" he asked.

I perked up. "Do you know where it is? I need to find it."

The boy gazed at me for a moment, then said, "Let's go to the rock."

He started toward the mouth of the cave, and I followed. Then he glanced back at the food. He leaned down, picked a couple of good roots from the pile, and handed them to me.

I hesitated. "But that's your food."

He nodded. "Mine to give."

The rock, big and flat, was on top of a hill near the cave. We sat on the edge of it with our feet dangling over the side. The sun shone on my face. After days of shade, it felt good.

I munched on the roots. "What's your name?"

"Sal."

"What is this place?"

"It's where we live," he said. "Me and my friends."

I thought of the other footprints and wondered how many friends he had.

Sal looked off toward the horizon. "You asked

about the City? It's over there."

I followed his gaze. "I don't see it."

"Behind those big trees. We don't go there."

I said, "Have you ever wondered about the people in the City?"

"I've heard about them," he said. "They do lots of things. They're always busy. They think they're in charge, but they're not."

He watched me closely to see how I'd react.

I said, "If they aren't in charge, who is?"

"Promise you won't tell?" he asked.

I nodded.

"Binders," he said.

The word sounded strange but familiar. I tried to think of where I'd heard it. For a moment I couldn't figure it out, and then I smiled. I hadn't just heard it; I had lived it. A Binder was a dreambender.

I tried not to show my surprise. "Who are they?"

"Wizards. Their faces are like flames. Their fingers are blades. They live in the clouds. When people do something wrong, the Binders reach down and fix it."

"Where did you hear this?" I asked.

He looked away. "It's a story. Someone told me. I don't remember who."

"Aren't you scared of them? These...Binders?"

He shook his head.

"Do you ever worry about them?" I said. "Do you ever dream about them?"

"What's a dream?" he asked.

# 13

## JEREMY

Sal's friends appeared that evening with more roots, berries, and flowers. They stared when they saw me, but Sal told them I was okay. After days of thrashing around in the woods, I felt good hearing him say it.

His friends put their food in the cave, then each took enough to eat and we sat around a fire that Sal had built. One of his friends had killed a rabbit. Sal put it on a stick and cooked it over the fire, then cut it into pieces with a knife and handed a piece to everybody, including me. I ate it, and it tasted good.

Sal liked visitors. That's what he told me. He used to live alone, then the others came, and pretty soon they changed from visitors into friends. They were a strange, mixed-up bunch.

There was a brother and sister named Zack and Deb, who except for Sal were the only ones who ever seemed to talk. There was a boy with one leg who walked using a crutch. One girl had a skinny dog, and the last girl must have been seven feet tall, with black, black hair and a white, white face.

As I watched them sit around the fire and eat, I thought about what Sal had told me. I turned to Deb, who was next to me. "Do you dream?"

She cocked her head. "Do I what?"

"Dream. You know—see stories and pictures when you're sleeping. They seem like real life until you wake up."

I looked around the circle. Their faces were blank. They had no idea what I was talking about.

"Pictures when you sleep?" said Deb. "That would be nice."

I said, "If you don't see pictures, what do you see?"

She shrugged and looked at the others. "Our eyes are closed. It's black, that's all."

Where I lived, everybody dreamed. Where Sal lived, nobody dreamed. What did it mean?

Sal and his friends roamed the woods, and the dreambenders didn't know where they were or if they were. The only way to meet them was in person, as I had. They had slipped off the dreamscape and between the cracks. They didn't exist. They were ghosts.

"How many of you are there?" I asked Sal.

He looked around the circle. "Six."

"No, I mean living in the woods. Not dreaming."

Deb giggled. "You ask funny questions."

"Why does it matter?" asked Sal.

Zack said, "We matter. This matters."

Sal got to his feet and disappeared inside the cave. He came out a moment later, holding a black thing that was wide and rounded at one end and narrow and straight at the other, the size of a child. Scratched and scuffed, it had a big dent on one side.

I noticed a crack that ran along the edge of the black thing, all the way around. Along one side of the crack were some metal pieces that must have been shiny once.

Sal tugged on one of them, and it flipped back with a snapping noise. He flipped the others, and the crack widened. The black thing was hollow. Something was in there.

Slowly, carefully, Sal swung back the top. The

black thing had been damaged, but it was just a holder to protect something else. It had done its job well.

Inside was a gleaming object made of wood, with a thin neck at one end and a curved, rounded body at the other. Strings stretched down the neck and across a hole in the body. There were six of them. Sal plucked one, and a note rang out.

Zack smiled. "Music matters."

I glanced around at the group. In my world, music wasn't a word you mentioned openly. You whispered it behind closed doors. Yet here was Zack, saying it and smiling. What kind of place was this?

Sal lifted the object out and set the black thing aside. Deb nodded toward the object.

"It's a sound box," she told me.

I asked Sal, "Where did you get it?"

"I found it in a tree. It was hanging like fruit."

Deb explained, "It was a floater. When the waters rose, it stayed on top. When the waters went down, it stuck in a tree."

Sal sat down and brushed his fingers across the strings. A wonderful sound came out. He poked his tongue from the corner of his mouth and did it again. Sal brushed the strings for a long time, and I listened. The sounds reminded me of the Meadow and of people I knew—they were thoughtful like Phillip, funny like Hannah, doubtful like Gracie, sure like Leif. I heard Arthur's encouragement and Dorothy's harsh judgment swirling like smoke above the flames.

"How do you do that?" I asked him.

He shrugged. "I just do."

Someone said, "It's a gift."

The voice was low and sweet. It rang like a gong. I looked around to see who had spoken.

It was the tall girl.

"All have gifts," she said. "Gifts make us special."

Dorothy had described dreambending as a gift. Were there other gifts? Did this odd group have them? Did I?

Four days ago I had left the Meadow sure of where I was going. Now my best hope of getting there was to rely on a group of misfits who ate berries and thought music was a gift. I thought of the singer, and suddenly I was eager to get going.

"Will you take me to the City?" I asked Sal.

The others stared at me. Sal studied the ground in front of him.

He murmured, "I told you, we don't go there."

"Then show me the way," I said. "You don't have to go. But I do."

Sal looked at the others. They didn't seem happy. He turned back to me.

"Why?"

It was a familiar question, one I'd been asking my whole life. I hadn't planned to tell anyone, but Sal had given me food and included me in his circle. He had played the sound box. I decided I owed him an answer.

"There's a girl," I said.

Deb grinned. I blushed.

I said, "It's not like that."

"What's it like?" she asked.

I thought of the dream. How do you explain colors to someone who can't see?

I said, "She lives in the City. She loves to sing. I need to find her."

Deb looked at the others. No one said anything. Then Zack turned to me.

"Need matters," he said.

The next morning, Sal took me to a big tree at the edge of the woods.

"This is as far as I go," he said. "Walk toward the sun and you'll reach the City."

Sal turned to leave, and I caught his arm. He looked back at me, his face smudged with dirt. Usually I knew people by their dreams. I knew Sal by what he had done.

"Thank you for helping me," I said.

He nodded. "I hope you find her."

"Clean your face sometime," I told him.

Sal laughed. Then he was gone.

# 14

## CALLIE

Freedom Day.

It was the biggest holiday of the year. On Freedom Day, businesses in the City closed and people filled the streets, celebrating freedom from pollution, destruction, and machines. Anyway, that's what my parents believed. For me it was simpler than that. It was a day off work, a time to have fun.

That morning I set the table, and my father whipped up some eggs. My mother baked a special kind of bread in a square pan and brought it to the table with a flourish.

"It's Freedom Bread," she told us as she sliced it. "My dad used to make it for the holiday. We looked forward to it every year. He cut it into three rows of three, like I'm doing, which always left a middle piece. There was nothing special about that piece, but to us kids it was the best. You know why?"

I studied the pan and saw it immediately. "There's just one."

"Right!" she said. "You wouldn't believe the fights we had over that middle piece. It used to drive my dad crazy."

My father chuckled. "Freedom to argue—the right of every kid."

She lifted out the middle piece and set it on my plate. "In our family there's no argument. Maybe it's why we only had one child."

I dug into the middle piece, which really was delicious. After breakfast I walked with my parents toward the Square. Several blocks from there, we started coming across groups of people, and soon we were in a happy crowd.

As we approached the Square, I heard a commotion off to one side. Looking over, I found myself staring at a banner. Splattered with color and hung on the side of a building, it said *Freedom to...* People of all ages were gathered around the banner, painting. Juanita stood nearby, talking to anyone who would listen. Eleesha and Pam worked next to the banner, handing out brushes and paint.

I touched my mother's shoulder. "I see someone I know. Why don't you and Dad go on ahead? I'll catch up with you."

My parents went on, and I made my way through the crowd to the banner. Eleesha grinned when she saw me.

"Callie! I didn't know if we'd see you again."

"Sorry..." I began, but she waved me off.

"Don't apologize. I'm just happy you're here."

I gestured toward the banner. "What's this?"

"Well," she said, "we love painting pictures, but for Freedom Day we wanted to do something more. You know, something that made a statement. Right, Pam?"

Pam, always the quiet one, nodded enthusiastically.

Eleesha said, "When people celebrate Freedom Day, they talk about freedom from—from fear, from hunger, from pollution, from war—as if freedom were a wall to keep us safe. But that's not what freedom means. It's a state of mind. It's a way of living. Yes, we love our freedom, but what do we do with it?"

Unable to contain herself, Pam blurted out, "Not freedom from. Freedom *to*!"

"Right," said Eleesha. "So we started a banner, and the people are helping us finish it. Look!"

A father held his baby son in one arm. With his free hand he was painting a word on the banner: *Build*.

An elderly woman stood with her husband. She smiled at him, then wrote the word *Love*.

A young man wearing a white shirt had used the paint to splash designs on his clothes and face, then had written *Be crazy!*

Other words covered the banner: *Run. Think. Disagree. Write. Pray. Help. Eat popcorn.*

"Well," said Eleesha, "what do you think?"

A feeling welled up inside me. On impulse, I approached the banner, took a brush, and dipped it in bright-red paint. With broad, bold strokes I wrote the word *Sing*.

Pam clapped. Eleesha gave me a hug and said, "It's perfect."

I put down the brush and stepped back, unsure of what I had done.

"You think so?" I asked.

"Absolutely," said Eleesha. "Tell you what. The three of us will mingle with the crowd. You can hand out brushes and paint."

It felt good to help. When people wrote their words, their faces lit up. I had never seen so many people smile.

Every so often I'd steal a glance at my word. Sometimes it glimmered in the sun. Sometimes I could barely read it. Sometimes it looked like blood.

I noticed a boy in the crowd. His clothes were strange to begin with but also wrinkled and torn. I thought he was watching me, but then he looked away. I stopped to help someone else, and when I turned back, he was standing next to me.

He stooped down, picked up a brush, and dabbed it in blue paint. He wrote on the banner: *Dream*. Then he looked back at me.

"We have to talk," he said.

# PART THREE

# THE SINGER

# 15

## CALLIE

The boy stared at me. His eyes were pleading.

"Why do we have to talk?" I asked.

"We just do."

I looked around. People were painting words on the banner and reading what others had painted. Eleesha and her friends spoke with the onlookers.

I said, "We can talk here. No one's listening."

He shook his head. "I don't like crowds."

I noticed that he was sweating, and he clenched and unclenched his hands. How can you live in the City and not like crowds?

"Let's stay here," I said. "I don't know you."

"But I know you," he said.

"You do?"

I tried to think of where we had met. At work maybe. On the street. I wondered if he had been following me.

"What's my name?" I asked.

"I…I don't know."

"This is getting strange," I said.

I turned to leave. He reached out and took my elbow. His touch was gentle.

"You're a singer," he said. "You work with numbers but don't like it."

I stared at him. "How did you know that?"

"It's hard to explain," he said.

"Try."

He took a deep breath. He closed his eyes for a moment. When he opened them, he seemed calmer.

He said, "You dream."

There was a disturbance off to our left. A young man was coming toward us through the crowd, his eyes glued to the boy. The young man was beautiful, with blond hair and a proud tilt to his chin. He wore the same odd clothes the boy was wearing.

The boy followed my gaze and saw the young man. He blanched.

"Leif!"

The boy stumbled backward, but the young man was too quick. He grabbed the boy's arm. "Time to go, Jeremy."

I didn't know what was happening, but it bothered me.

"Who are you?" I asked the young man.

"A friend," he said.

The boy tried to pull free. "Yes, we're friends, but—"

"Jeremy's troubled," said the young man. "He always has been. Sorry about this."

He gripped Jeremy's arm and started to drag him off. Jeremy tried to get loose but couldn't.

Suddenly Eleesha was at my side. "What's going on?"

Jeremy struggled. He reached toward me with his free arm as if he were drowning. His gaze fastened onto mine.

"You're on a mountain, and there are doors," he said. "Behind them are your parents and a mirror."

Leif tried to cover Jeremy's mouth but couldn't.

"Why is he doing that?" asked Eleesha.

As Leif took him away, Jeremy called out to me, "You hear singing. You hurry down the mountain."

A picture was forming in my mind. I had seen it before but somehow I'd forgotten it. A woman sat on a patch of grass, her head thrown back, singing from the depths of her heart.

I was the woman.

Joy washed over me.

"Stop him," I whispered.

Eleesha turned to me.

"Stop him!" I said.

Quick as a shot, Eleesha took off after them, shoving people aside. When she reached them, she lowered her shoulder and rammed into Leif. Grunting, he loosened his grip just enough for Jeremy to pull free. Leif tried to stop him, but Eleesha dove for Leif's knees and tackled him.

"Go!" she yelled.

I grabbed Jeremy's hand, and we took off running through the crowd.

* * *

Whenever I wanted a break from work, I would slip outside and explore the City. One of my favorite places was a little courtyard a short distance from the Square. If you didn't know it was there, you'd never find it. One day I had seen a man emerge from the courtyard. Curious, I had discovered the entrance. There was a bench, and in the mornings, the sun shone between the buildings to light up a little patch of grass, the only one for blocks.

I would sit on the bench and gaze at the grass. Sometimes I would get on my hands and knees to look. Worms wriggled. Bugs crawled. Ants labored, all in that little patch of grass. Once I saw a butterfly. It landed on the grass and balanced, its wings beating slowly.

Where did the creatures come from? Where had they been? How did they end up here?

I took Jeremy to the courtyard. Winded, frightened, he sat beside me on the bench. I had a hundred questions for him and was surprised at the first one I asked.

"Have you ever seen grass like this?"

He glanced at me and burst out laughing as if it had been pent up inside him for a long time. I laughed too. It felt good.

"Why are we laughing?" I asked.

He said, "Where I come from, grass is everywhere. You can hardly take a step without squashing a worm."

"Is there such a place?"

He looked away. He crossed and uncrossed his arms, then chewed on a thumbnail.

Finally he looked back.

"It's called the Meadow," he said. "It's a long way from here."

"Is it in the land of Between?" I asked.

He shook his head and leaned forward. "You remember that guy who was chasing me?"

"Leif?"

"Right. Leif once asked me the strangest question: Between what? He said if the place is called Between, there must be something on each side. Makes sense, doesn't it? Somehow, it had never occurred to me."

"Me neither," I said.

"Well, now I know, and you will too. The City's on one side and the Meadow's on the other. That's why they call it Between."

It was so obvious, I had to giggle. "I feel stupid. Maybe we're both stupid."

He grinned. "I might start liking you. But I still don't know your name."

Somehow it seemed okay to tell him.

"Callie Crawford," I said.

"I'm Jeremy Finn."

He looked around, as if checking to make sure no one would hear. Then, in a low voice, he told me, "They don't want us to figure it out. People in the City can't know about the Meadow. People in the Meadow can't come to the City."

"Why not?" I asked.

He said, "You may not believe it."

"Try me," I said.

# 16

## JEREMY

How had Leif found the City?

Maybe he had guessed. Maybe the fixers had told him. He had always been a smart kid—smart about figuring things out, tracking things down, making sure things were right. And I, the kid at the head of the class, was the dummy.

Leif was a born fixer, and they knew it. I wondered if this was his first assignment. Remembering his stern gaze and iron grip, I doubted it.

"Now tell me," said Callie.

I was sitting on a bench in the tiny, cramped courtyard she thought of as a wide-open space. I was miles from home, breaking the law, running away, and didn't have the beginnings of a plan. I had wanted to see the singer. That was all—not in my head or in a mirror, but in the world. In life. I hadn't planned anything more. But when I finally saw her, it hadn't been enough.

I had seen her. I had heard her. Now I needed to tell her. So I did.

How do you describe a dreambender? How do you explain what it's like to go inside people's heads and shift things around? It sounds impossible. When you say it out loud, it sounds wrong.

Callie didn't want to believe me, but she had heard my description of her dream. I had been there, and she knew it. I was like a prowler, going through her private possessions. It seemed shameful, but I'd been doing it for weeks, and they had praised me for my skill.

"You saw my dream?" she said, still trying to understand. "Then you changed it?"

"I didn't. They did. It's what we do in the Meadow."

"Why?"

"To solve problems. To make the world better."

"By changing dreams?"

I said, "Dreams begin all things, good and bad."

*The Book of Raines*, chapter one. Leif would have been proud.

"You can't control people like that," said Callie.

"We do. We have for years."

"Since the Warming?"

I nodded. "Because of the Warming. We can never allow it to happen again."

"How many of you are there?"

"A few hundred. Not many."

She glanced around us at the buildings, and so did I. Suddenly they seemed like props in one of the plays we had put on as kids—sticks and canvas, nothing more.

"It's wrong," I said.

She snorted. "No kidding."

"That's why I came. They told me to bend your dream, so you'd be a computer. But I wouldn't do it. I wanted you to sing."

"You broke the rules?" she asked.

"For a day. Then they found out and punished me. I'm banned from the dreamscape for a year."

"For me?" She gazed at me thoughtfully. Then she looked off into the distance and smiled. "I remember that day. I wish all days could be like that."

Of course, that was the problem. Her days couldn't be like that—not all of them, maybe not any of them.

"The dreambenders will stop you," I told her. "They'll bend your dreams. If one of them can't do it, another one will. If that doesn't work, there are always the fixers."

"The fixers?"

"When a dreambender breaks the rules like I did, the fixers take care of it. Leif is one of them."

I pictured Leif's face. His expression looked the same as it used to, but somehow it was different—tougher, harder. He had already been on my trail, and now, thanks to my brilliant moves, he was on Callie's too. I had wanted to see her, and I had put her in danger.

I said, "They'll be coming soon. I need to go."

"That's crazy," she said. "You don't know the City. They'll find you."

"Look, Callie," I said, "where I come from we have three rules: 'Never meet the dreamer. Never harm the dreamer. Always follow the Plan.' I've broken two of them, and I don't want to break the third."

"You didn't harm me," she said. "You told me about the dreambenders. You've given me a gift."

*Gift.* It was the word Dorothy and Arthur had used to describe my dreambending. The tall girl had used it when talking about Sal. What was a gift? If it hurt you, was it still a gift?

I climbed to my feet. "I'll get you in trouble. You stay here."

"And do what?" she said. "Go back to computing? Sit at a desk? Sneak away to look at the sun? Take off once a year to celebrate Freedom Day? What kind of life is that?"

"Maybe it's a good life. The dreambenders think so."

Her eyes flashed. "While they lounge on the grass, stealing people's dreams."

"They're not like that."

"Jeremy, you ran away from them. Why are you defending them?"

I met her gaze, then looked away. "I'm not sure."

"You know," she said, "I've always thought there was something wonderful beyond the City and, if I looked hard enough, maybe I could find it. You helped me see it. You pulled back the curtain. It was just one day, one glimpse, but it was enough. I need to see what's out there. You could show me."

Watching Callie, I could see why City people were never supposed to learn about the Meadow. They might start wondering. They might start hoping. And hope, as Arthur had explained, was strong.

"What about your family?" I said. "You can't just leave them."

"They'll be sad. But they'll understand."

There was a look in her eyes. It was excitement and anger and determination all mixed together.

Callie was on a journey, and so was I. At one end of my journey was the Meadow, a place where I felt strong and sure. The other end was a mystery. It might be good. It might be bad. It was probably dangerous. But it was where I wanted to go. I was traveling down a path, away from home. Away from plans. Away from comfort, with a girl I didn't know.

"Why are you staring at me?" she asked.

"Sorry," I mumbled.

"Look, I'm glad you're trying to help me. I'm grateful. But knowing my dreams isn't the same as knowing me. It doesn't give you the right to make my decisions. That's my job."

She sat there for a moment, lost in thought. Then suddenly she stood up.

"Let's go."

"Where?" I asked.

"Between."

# 17

## CALLIE

We slept in Between that night. It was thrilling and frightening. I was used to buildings, and they were gone. Trees surrounded the clearing where we had slept.

I had dreamed about Between since I was little—all of us had. In the dreams, terrible things happened to people who went there. Trees crushed them. Vines grabbed them and pulled them under. Most of us had ventured inside once or twice, of course, just to say we'd done it. But the dreams were terrifying, so we learned to stay away.

It still scared me, but now I needed a place to think and time to do it. Between was the obvious choice. Besides, I was starting to think that maybe dreambenders had planted the nightmares. Maybe they were trying to keep me out of Between. That made me want to stay, at least for a while.

I shivered. Overhead, stars winked.

"There are more stars here," I told Jeremy.

He lay next to me on the ground, gazing upward. He was relaxed now, in a way that he hadn't been in the City.

"They're just brighter," he said. "The darker the sky, the brighter the stars. They're the same ones though, no matter where you are. When I left the Meadow, it was one of the things that kept me going. The stars reminded me of home."

I thought of my own home in the City. My parents were there. By now they had gotten my note. I had wanted to go with Jeremy, but not without telling them. The note hadn't said much—just that I was safe and that, no matter what anyone told them, I was doing the right thing. They were worried, I was sure. But I knew they loved me.

I remembered the way Eleesha had thrown herself at the young man named Leif. She hadn't hesitated, and I wondered why. Maybe it was because of what she had shared at the cemetery about her brother. Did it make us friends? But now, like Eleesha's brother, I was gone. I had left her behind. I hoped she would understand.

When Jeremy and I had hurried from the courtyard, we had made our way to my house. I'd written the note, then we'd put clothes, a blanket, and some other things into a backpack and headed for the trees. There had been no sign of Leif, so far at least.

"I've never seen a night this dark," I said, looking up into the moonless sky.

"Isn't it wonderful?"

"You like it?" I asked.

He looked over at me, shocked. "You don't?"

I said, "Darkness is scary. You can't see anything."

"That's not true," he said. "It's when you see the most."

I wondered what he could possibly mean, and then I remembered.

"Dreams," I said. "You see dreams. What's it like?"

He thought for a moment, then said, "What's water like? What's air like? They just are."

"Do you like seeing them?" I asked.

"Yes."

"Do you like changing them?"

"I did. Now I'm not so sure. But sometimes it

can help."

"And who's the judge of that?" I asked. I could hear an edge in my voice.

"We are, I guess," he admitted. "Look, I know you don't approve of what dreambenders do. Sometimes I don't either. But it can be a good thing. You should see what people dream—terrible things, awful things. Sometimes people get stuck in a dream and can't get free. We help them."

His face, strange and kind, was pale in the starlight. Watching him, I wondered what the other dreambenders were like. I had been thinking of them as meddlers, trespassers. But I could see that they saw themselves as helpers. They were taking care of us. Some of my neighbors in the City kept animals and called them pets. Maybe we were pets too.

"Can you look at a dream right now, while we're lying here?" I asked Jeremy.

He shook his head. "I'm not allowed. It's part of my punishment. They'd know I was there."

"Are you allowed to dream?" I asked.

"Sure," he said, "but I don't dream much. When I do, the dreambenders see them—yours too."

A chill ran down my back. I pulled up the blanket,

turned over, and closed my eyes.

*Try not to dream*, I thought.

* * *

When I woke up, we were surrounded.

There were six of them, led by a tall, lanky, dark-skinned boy with eyes that took in everything. At first I was frightened, but there was something about the dark-skinned boy that seemed familiar and reassuring. I studied the others, who included a one-legged boy and a girl with the skinniest dog I'd ever seen. They were just standing there, watching us.

I poked Jeremy and whispered, "Wake up."

He opened his eyes.

"We have visitors," I said.

Jeremy looked at the dark-skinned boy and smiled. "Hey, Sal."

"You found her," said the boy.

"You know these people?" I asked Jeremy.

"Don't turn your back on them," he said. "They might give you food."

Next to Sal was a young woman who towered over everybody, and beside her were two people who looked alike except one was a boy and one was a girl.

"Food matters," said the boy. "Sleep matters."

The girl told me, "That means hello, glad to meet you. He's Zack. I'm Deb. I'd introduce you to our friends, but we don't know their names."

Friends without names, I thought. What kind of place is this?

Jeremy turned to Sal. "How did you know we were here?"

"I didn't. She did."

Sal signaled, and the girl with the skinny dog stepped out from between the trees.

"She's our lookout," he explained. "She knows when people come and go. She's always roaming around, out of sight."

Sal eyed me, curious. Jeremy said, "Oh, sorry. This is Callie. Callie, these are some people I met."

"You're from the City," said Sal.

"Is it that obvious?" I asked.

Deb said, "I like your blanket." She knelt and ran her hand across the top of it. "It's soft."

My stomach growled. I said, "Could I have some of that food now?"

Sal led us beneath trees and over hills. His friends followed happily, while Jeremy and I labored along behind, huffing and puffing. The two of us led very different lives, but we had one thing in common: we didn't get much exercise.

After what seemed like a long time, we arrived at a cave. Deb built a fire in front, and the others gathered around, all but the girl with the skinny dog, who slipped off among the trees. Sal went inside the cave and came back a moment later with a rough bowl full of berries, along with flowers and some gnarled, lumpy things that looked like bark. Jeremy took two of the lumpy things and handed one to me.

"Try it," he said. "It's good."

I eyed it and decided it probably was if you were a beaver. I didn't want to be rude though, so I nibbled the edge of it. Amazingly, he was right.

As I ate, Jeremy told me what little he knew about Sal and his friends, including the fact that they didn't dream.

"So the dreambenders don't know about them?" I asked.

"I guess not," he said.

I asked Sal and the others how they spent their time, and they told me. As far as I could tell, their lives didn't have a purpose or pattern. They ate.

They slept. They explored the woods. They gathered food. Some days, they didn't do anything.

I have to admit, it bothered me. In the City we always had a purpose. I was a computer. Everything I did revolved around that fact. I didn't necessarily like it, but it seemed right, or at least it had before. We also had history. It made us who we were. Who were Sal and his friends?

How did they know if all they thought about was today? If I stayed in Between, would I end up like them? A part of me liked the idea. Maybe I'd get used to it. I could wander through the woods like Sal and his friends. I could be free.

When we finished eating, Sal went into the cave and came out holding a wooden object that he called a sound box. He sat down beside the fire, cradled the sound box in his lap, and ran his fingers across the strings.

Music came out. It was like singing but with a different voice. The voice was wise and good. It had colors—red, green, yellow. Sometimes the colors were bright. Sometimes they were soft and dark, like the forest at sunset.

I thought I had met Sal in the woods, but I

hadn't. This was the real Sal. You had to listen to know him. What I heard wasn't ideas or plans or calculations. It was feelings and hopes. It was longing. It was pure emotion.

One melody caught my attention. It was sad but somehow full of joy. It seemed to be asking questions, and I wanted to answer. So I began to sing. There were no words, just a song that wrapped itself over, under, and around Sal's music.

The others stared at me, but at first I didn't notice. I had sung in the dream, and sunlight had washed over me. I felt the sunlight again. I was in the dream, but it was real. I stood up and walked toward Sal. He gazed at me, motionless except for the hand that kept strumming, strumming.

I stood before him, and music poured out of me. The trees vanished. The cave and the path collapsed, forming a tunnel to the clouds. Inside it were me and the music and Sal, or the part of Sal made of notes and phrases, the part I could feel.

There was no day or night, no hours or minutes. There was now, stretching forward and backward forever. I wasn't Callie. I wasn't a computer. I was the song, and the song was me.

# 18

## CALLIE

Later, sitting around the fire, I asked Sal where he had found the sound box.

"In a tree," he said. He told me about the day he had found it and how he had taught himself to play.

As he spoke, I looked around. Sticks, tools, and other objects were scattered on the ground. The cave entrance yawned, cool and dark.

I said, "What is this place?"

"Maybe Boogey lives here," said Jeremy.

"Boogey?"

Jeremy smiled. "He's not real. Where I come from, the adults make up stories about him to scare us and make us behave."

"Stories matter," said Zack. He glanced at Deb,

worried. For someone who didn't talk much, he said a lot. He had an odd way of expressing himself. Things "mattered"—food, sleep, stories. I think he meant they were important.

Deb told me, "Just because it's a story doesn't mean it isn't real."

I thought about that one for a minute. At the computing center, they would say she was wrong. In Between, I wasn't so sure.

"You tell stories?" I asked her. "Like what?"

Deb said, "The Tree That Kept Giving. The Day of Seven Suns. Moses and the Ark."

"I know that one!" I said.

"The Music Place," said Sal. "That's my favorite story."

Suddenly I was back at the Midway, looking over Pam's shoulder at her painting. *The Music Place*. That's what she had called it.

"Can we hear the story?" I asked.

Deb looked around the circle. The others smiled. The tall girl nodded.

Sal played softly on the sound box, and Deb began the story.

"Once, before the Warming," she said, "the

world was filled with music. People sang as often as they talked. They tapped out rhythms on wood. They squeezed notes from metal pipes. They pulled strings tight and made them vibrate. Music was everywhere.

"Sometimes, on special days, groups of people would gather and make music together. Some would play, and the rest would listen. If the music was good, the listeners would clap their hands to show they liked it."

I imagined a group of people like me but different. Some sang. Some held strange objects and used them to make music. I wanted to be there with them, to live in a world where music was as important as computing.

"There was a big building made for music," Deb went on, "with tall ceilings and glittering lights."

"The Music Place," said Sal.

"What did it look like?" I asked.

Deb smiled. "It wasn't like other buildings. The inside was wood. The outside was metal, with points and curves."

I had seen the building in Pam's painting. At the time I had assumed she'd made it up. Now I wondered.

"Is it real?" I asked her.

Deb glanced at Sal, and he looked away. As he did, the girl with the skinny dog came bursting from the trees.

"People are coming!" she said. "Run!"

I glanced at Jeremy. He knew who was coming, and so did I. It was Leif and the fixers.

Sal stowed the sound box, and we took off into the woods. The tall girl led the way, holding a sharp stick. The boy with one leg was behind her, leaning on Zack's shoulder. Deb went next, with the food. Jeremy and I stuck close to Sal. Following behind, keeping watch, was the girl with the skinny dog.

The fixers scared me, and I could tell Jeremy was scared too. Leif claimed to be Jeremy's friend, but I wondered what that meant.

I heard a shout. The fixers had reached the cave. We kept moving to stay ahead of them.

We had tried not to leave a trail, but we had left in a hurry. A few moments later, we heard them coming through the bushes. The sound got louder. They had found our trail and were catching up.

Jeremy, already out of breath, glanced over at Sal. "I brought them here. I'm sorry."

"What do you think they'll do?" I asked him.

"Take us back. You'll compute. I'll dig ditches." He tried to smile.

"It's not funny," I said.

Jeremy turned to Sal. "Leave us here. You can get away. We'll tell them we found the cave and built the fire."

Sal grinned, then realized Jeremy was serious. Jeremy really thought the fixers would believe him. Maybe they would.

"No," said the tall girl. "We'll stay together."

Jeremy and I looked at her in surprise. We hadn't known she was listening. Studying her, I realized that the tall girl was always listening.

I started to object, but Sal stopped me. "Save your energy," he said. "You'll need it."

He was right. Already we were slowing down. The boy with one leg had trouble keeping up. Jeremy and I were getting tired.

I watched as Sal looked for places to hide. There was a boulder, but it wasn't big enough. Mostly, there were trees.

Sal told us his idea. His friends picked out some trees and scrambled up, quickly and easily, even the one-legged boy. Noticing that we needed help, Sal clasped his hands and offered them to me. I stepped on hesitantly and struggled to a low branch. Jeremy followed, skinning his elbows and knees. Finally we found a place on the branch to stand. Our legs were quivering. Jeremy's face, red a moment before, was pale. Sal shinnied up behind us just in time.

The boy called Leif led the group. There were four other fixers, men and women dressed in the same odd clothes Jeremy wore. They pounded along beneath the trees, looking right and left, forward and back. It was obvious they didn't live in the woods. If they had, they would have known to look up too.

Leif stopped and studied the ground. When the others hurried off, he yelled to them, "I'm coming. Wait for me!"

A moment later he was gone. To be safe, we stayed in the trees a long time. Then we climbed down, with Sal helping Jeremy and me. We gathered beneath a tree.

"Now what?" Jeremy asked Sal.

"We could go back to the cave," said Deb.

Sal shook his head. "They might be watching it."

"We can't just run," said Jeremy. "We need somewhere to go."

I watched Sal. He hesitated, thinking. For a second he looked worried. Then he seemed to make a decision.

"Let's go to the Music Place," he said.

I gaped at him. "It's real? It's not just a story?"

He showed a hint of a smile. "You'll see."

# 19

## JEREMY

As we hurried through the woods, my mind ran ahead of me.

What was I doing? I had wanted to meet the singer, and I had done it. Since then, I'd been going on instinct, running blind. I was used to living in my head, watching pictures, and suddenly there were arms and legs, hands and feet. Lips.

I glanced at Callie moving along beside me, a computer who wanted to be a singer.

Maybe she was a singer. Maybe I was an outlaw. I knew what Leif thought and had a pretty good idea how he was feeling. Leif had a temper. He didn't like to lose at anything. When he was given a job, he did it. Now I was the job.

"Are you okay?" asked Callie.

"Yeah," I mumbled.

"We'll be fine, Jeremy. You'll see."

*We*. I had noticed the word when Callie had used it before. That time, she had meant the two of us. Now she was talking about Sal and his friends. Who was *we*? I used to think *we* were the dreambenders, and *they* were the City people. Then I learned there were people in Between.

Were they a we? Was I part of it? I thought of all the people I'd seen since leaving the Meadow, and I wondered if somehow all of them might be one big *we*—me, Callie, Sal and his friends, Leif, the dreambenders, the crowds of strangers in the City. If they were we, who was I? Where did I fit in? Where would I go?

To the Music Place, Sal had said.

Callie had asked if the Music Place was real. I wondered about that. I wondered about a lot of things—Callie, dreambenders, Between, and now Sal and his friends. I didn't think they would mislead us, but did that mean they knew where they were going? Were we crazy to follow?

We were living a story, chasing a legend. I

thought of Dorothy and Arthur. I knew what they would say. We were fools. We were dangerous to ourselves and others.

Sal led the way, with Callie at his side. The rest of us followed. Behind us, silent, out of sight, lurked the girl with the skinny dog, keeping watch.

I wish I could say which direction Sal headed, but it all looked the same to me. As far as I could tell, there was no trail. But Sal seemed to know exactly where he was going.

Whatever direction it was, we were surrounded by trees. I began to wish I had never seen one. They were everywhere, thousands of them, hemming us in, reaching for us, rustling in the breeze. I didn't like the tall buildings and walls in the City, but at least they didn't move. They weren't alive and growing.

I found myself longing for the Meadow, with its open spaces and high clouds. I remembered the approach of evening, the way the sun would settle on the horizon and slowly dissolve, like butter in a dish. The sky would turn orange and pink and red, then a deep purple.

Darkness would come, and dreams would start. It seemed so beautiful and so far away.

I realized that the woods were getting darker. Somewhere behind the trees, the sky was changing colors.

"Shouldn't we stop for the night?" I asked.

Callie shook her head. "Let's keep going."

Soon we had no choice. In the dim light, Sal somehow spotted a small clearing, and we made our way there. I plopped down on a fallen tree. It felt good to rest. Callie paced the area, agitated.

"Are we getting close?" she asked Sal.

"You'll see," he told her again.

We didn't build a fire, because the fixers might have seen the smoke. Deb passed out food. We ate in silence, then stretched out on the ground. There was no moon. The woods grew darker by the minute. Faces faded and flickered out, leaving us alone with our fears.

I had too many to count. I feared losing the dreamscape, being cut off from the dreambenders, never again seeing Hannah laugh or Gracie bite her lip. I feared for Callie. I had raised her hopes, and now they were all she had. She had turned her back on the rest—her family, her job, her life. She had followed me, and I had no idea where I was going.

She stopped pacing. I stretched out on the ground, and she lay down next to me.

"Jeremy?" she whispered.

"Yes."

"What are you thinking about?"

"You," I said.

I was surprised to feel her snuggle up closer. She was warm and soft.

"What's going to happen to me?" she asked.

I thought about it some more. "I'm not sure. Whatever it is though, it belongs to you—not your parents, not the dreambenders, not me. Good or bad, it's yours."

I couldn't see her face, but I think she smiled. A few minutes later, she was asleep.

I looked up between the branches at the stars. In the Meadow, the stars had seemed like friends. Earlier in Between, they had been my guide. Now somehow, unsure of where we were going, I saw them as cold and distant. The more I ran, the farther away they seemed.

How long could we run? How many paths could we take? Where could we hide? If we didn't find the Music Place, what would we do? If we found it, what would we do?

Even if we managed to escape, what would happen to the people in the City? They believed they were free, but they weren't. I remembered Yolanda, one of Arthur's watcher friends. She had a pet, a beautiful green bird that she called a parakeet. I was amazed at the way the bird always stayed with her, perched on Yolanda's shoulder. Then one day, Arthur told me why. There's a way that wings can be clipped so the bird looks the same but can't fly.

The dreambenders had clipped the wings of the City people. We had told ourselves it made the world a better place, but did it?

Was it good to bend dreams? Was it right to block hopes? Was it fair for a small group, no matter how kind or well-meaning, to control the world?

It seemed that all I had was questions. Once, Dorothy had said the questions could get me into trouble but could also help me. I wondered how. They just led to more questions, spiraling into the sky, beautiful but useless.

Unless.

What if the answer to my questions wasn't words but action? I could do something. If I didn't like the way the City people were being treated, I could try to change it. Callie was changing. She had risked everything. So could I. But I couldn't do it in Between.

I could do it in the dreamscape.

The thought clicked into place like the missing piece of a puzzle. The answer had been there all along, waiting for me to see it and take it.

I was a dreambender. The dreamscape was where I lived. I'd been exploring the other world, but it had never seemed as real. In the dreamscape, the feelings were deeper. The pictures were stranger and more vivid. I was banned from going there by the Council. But the Council was wrong.

My problems had started in the dreamscape. To solve them, I needed to go back. There was no other way.

I could return to the dreamscape.

I could confront Dorothy and the watchers.

It was time to stop running.

# 20

## JEREMY

It was there. It had been there all along. All I had to do was close my eyes and go.

The trees went away. So did Callie and the others. The sky glowed, but it wasn't the sky.

It was a kind of screen. Pictures flickered across it. I watched, as I had since I was a child.

The dreambenders would know I was there, but maybe not right away. They were busy with other things—captivated, as we always were. Watching dreams was like looking into someone's heart. It was magnificent, and it was awful. How had I lived without it?

While I waited, I roamed from dream to dream. I saw things that were simple and terrifying.

A man drank a cup of coffee. A boa constrictor wrapped around a young girl's body. Blood rained from the clouds. A woman was trapped in a box and couldn't get out. Silver balls clicked together steadily, hypnotically. Crowds of people floated into the air and swarmed like gnats. A dog turned into a lily, and the lily into a coin.

A machine shaped like a giant wheel rotated, carrying cars full of people into the air and back down again. I had seen machines in the dreamscape, but this was a new one. Machine dreams had to be bent and, sure enough, I felt a dreambender approach. The scene shifted and the wheel dissolved, leaving a child's toy. A little boy picked it up, disappointed but not knowing why.

The mind began to drift away, then stopped. The dreambender had noticed me. Before I could blink, there was another and another. They clustered around, their thoughts buzzing. They knew who I was and what I had done. I was banned—how could I return? There was shock, disappointment, anger. In the midst of it, a voice emerged.

"Hello, Jeremy." It was Dorothy.

"I wondered how long it would take," I said.

"Why did you do it?" she said.

"Which part?"

"All of it. Running away. Breaking the rules. Meeting the dreamer. Returning to a place where you're not allowed."

"I have some questions," I said.

"You always do."

"These are important."

Her voice pulsed sadly. "As important as the group? As the world?"

I said, "How did it get to be like this?"

"Like what?"

"Dreams are wonderful. Why do we use them as weapons?"

"Weapons hurt," said Dorothy. "We help."

"We use them to rule the world."

"You really believe that?"

I smiled. "Now you're the one asking questions."

"We don't rule the world," said Dorothy. "We shape it. We support it."

"We bend it," I said. "The world is bent. It's crooked, twisted, hunched over."

"It's safe."

I remembered the wild vegetation of Between

and the hubbub of the City. “We made a trade. We gave up hope for safety. And it wasn’t ours to give.”

There was a fluttering in the dreamscape, a crush of thoughts and feelings. I could tell that it bothered Dorothy.

“You think all of us should break the rules?” she asked.

Suddenly I was a child again, listening to Dorothy in class. “You know what I mean.”

“We follow the Document,” she said. “It’s a framework. It’s a place to live, like a house.”

“Like a jail,” I said.

I could see Dorothy’s anger flare as surely as if she’d been standing in front of me.

“What is it you want?” she asked.

“We need to change,” I said. “We can’t keep going like this.”

“Everything’s fine. The Warming is over, and it won’t come again. We’ve made sure of that.”

“I met the dreamer. Her name is Callie.”

I heard sounds of shock and fear. Dorothy, as chairman of the Council, had certainly been told by the fixers that I’d met Callie, but the others didn’t know.

"Arthur called her a computer, but she's not," I said. "She's a singer. She's beautiful."

"You've tinkered with things you don't understand," said Dorothy.

"Singing makes her happy. Numbers don't."

"You have no idea what you're doing."

"I told her about us."

It was one thing to defy the dreambenders; telling a dreamer about them was another thing entirely. I had given away our great secret.

I could feel Dorothy shudder. "Oh, Jeremy."

"We've got to tell them," I said. "All of them."

"You would do that?" she asked in a tired voice.

"I've met the City people. They think they love freedom, but they don't know what it is. It's time for us to tell them. You should do it. But if you won't, I will."

Dorothy snapped, "What happened to your questions? I can think of some good ones. What if it all goes wrong? What if it blows up in our faces? Why do we think the world will turn out any different this time? Have we really changed that much? Would there be another Warming? Are you ready to betray everything the dreambenders have worked for—hundreds of them, going back to Carlton

Raines? What about them?"

"We betray the City people every day," I said.

I tried to sound strong, but Dorothy's questions made me wonder. Was I doing the right thing? What if my idea was a mistake?

"Maybe it's not too late," said Dorothy. "You were our shining star, our greatest hope. You still could be."

"Me?"

"You can be a great leader, Jeremy."

"I can?"

I had expected punishment, banishment, swift and final. Not this.

"You're special," said Dorothy. "You have unique gifts; we've always known that. Come home, Jeremy. Come back to the Meadow. Join us. Lead us. Make us strong."

I imagined myself in the cottage, looking over the Plan, skimming across the water with the watchers, directing them as they gave assignments, helping a young dreambender the way Arthur had helped me.

I imagined Callie singing.

"No," I said. "It's too late. Too much has happened."

Dorothy sighed. Her mind closed in on me. The others followed. Since we were in the dreamscape, I wasn't sure what they could do. Trap me? Catch me? Imprison me? I didn't know and didn't want to find out.

So once again, reluctantly, I ran.

How do you run in the dreamscape? I wasn't sure. I just knew I was moving away, and I hoped it was fast enough to escape. Dreams sped by. I reached out and felt them with my mind, woven strands waiting to be untied. I could adjust them. I could be the greatest dreambender—greater than Arthur, greater than Dorothy. I could be the next Carlton Raines. I flung the thought aside and kept moving.

I became aware of the sound I had imagined just a moment before. It had drawn me in from the beginning, pulling me through the dreamscape, to Between, to the crowds in the City and beyond. It was my beacon and my hope. Callie was singing.

A lake came into view. Callie's voice floated over the water. I thought of her asleep beneath the trees in Between, and I knew she was having a dream.

I followed her voice. It was coming from the other side of the lake. Behind me, Dorothy called,

"Jeremy, where are you? Come back. We can talk."

I kept going, around the lake and toward Callie. As I ran, the sun broke through, and suddenly there she was, singing beside the lake the way I'd seen her that very first time.

When I reached her, she smiled and paused. "You're in my dream. How did you get here?"

"Through the dreamscape."

Callie took my hand. She ran her fingers over my cheek. Then she kissed me. It felt as natural as a warm breeze. She held me. We sat there, strangers in a land that was familiar and new.

"Jeremy, wake up."

I opened my eyes. The lake was gone. I was in Between, and it was morning. Beyond the tree branches, the sky was turning orange. Callie looked down at me.

"You were in the dreamscape," she said. "I thought you were banned."

"I was. But I went back and talked to Dorothy. I tried to convince her the dreambenders were wrong. She didn't get mad. She didn't arrest me. Instead, she did something amazing. She asked if I would be their leader."

"Leader? Of the dreambenders?"

I nodded. "It scared me."

"Why?"

"Because I wanted to say yes."

I realized that I was shaking. I couldn't tell if I was frightened or just cold.

Callie put her arm around me. She touched my lips and kissed me. It was like the dream but different. The kiss felt warm and soft, but it was solid, something I could count on.

After a while, I looked around. Sal and the others were getting ready. I struggled to my feet. "We need to get going."

Sal set off once again, and we followed. There was no trail, but he seemed to know exactly where he was going. We trudged along all morning. When the sun was overhead, we stopped to eat some food that Deb and Zack had brought, then set off again.

Sometime later, I spotted something in the distance that looked like a wall. As we got closer, I realized that it was a huge stone cliff extending in both directions as far as I could see.

I asked Sal, "Can we go around it?"

"No," he said.

"Well, we can't climb over it," I said.

"That's right."

"Then what do we do?"

"You'll see," he said.

"'You'll see'? You keep saying that. What does it mean? Where are you taking us?"

Sal gazed at me calmly. Maybe if you don't dream or worry, you can be calm. But I couldn't.

I said, "Tell us. Please."

"We're not going around the cliff or over it," he said. "We're going through it."

# 21

## CALLIE

The Music Place was real. With all my heart I wanted to believe it. I needed to believe it. But as I approached the cliff with the others, my heart sank. The journey—*our* journey, Jeremy's and mine—seemed to have come to an end. It had hit a wall. The wall was immense and impenetrable.

How could we go through it? What did Sal mean? Maybe Sal and his friends were misfits and nothing more after all, living in the moment, confusing stories with reality.

I took Jeremy's hand. We watched as Sal walked up to the cliff. He inspected its surface, moving along it until he found what he was looking for.

Then he took one step and disappeared.

I looked at Jeremy. He looked back at me. Then he hurried to the place where Sal had stood.

He disappeared too.

Deb grinned. "Isn't it amazing?"

She led me to the wall and showed me the place where Sal and Jeremy had been standing. There was a tall, vertical crack in the rough stone surface that I could only see close up. I knew I could squeeze into the crack if I approached it at the right angle, and that's what Deb did. I took a deep breath and followed, with the others right behind.

We sidestepped perhaps fifty yards, and then the crack widened to reveal a narrow trail. We followed it single file up a series of switchbacks. Soon, out of breath, I was standing with Jeremy, next to Sal and his friends at the top of the cliff. The land of Between stretched out beneath us, a solid carpet of treetops. Far off in the distance, I could make out a few tall buildings in the City.

I heard something in the distance, like the hooting of an owl but different. It was higher and sweeter. There were lots of notes, dozens of them, each round and bright and perfect.

"Did you hear that?" I asked Jeremy.

"Hear what?"

"Sounds."

Or echoes of sounds, memories of sounds, barely loud enough to notice. I stepped away from the cliff and headed toward them.

Jeremy said, "We should stay together."

I kept walking. "Then come with me."

The top of the cliff was a forest, like Between but somehow different. There were trees and a path. We picked our way through bushes and vines, stepping over them, going around them, always moving forward. For a while it seemed as if the sounds weren't getting any louder. Finally I noticed a change. About that same time, Jeremy perked up.

"I hear it!" He turned to me. "What is it?"

"A song," I said.

I became aware of another sound behind and below the song. It was a stream. Rounding a tree, I saw water flowing down a hill. Beside the stream was a rock, and on the rock sat a woman.

She was tiny but seemed big. She was old but seemed young. Her eyes were closed, but I could swear she saw me.

She wore the plainest of clothes, if you could call

them that. They appeared to have been stitched together from bags. Her hair was long and gray. Her feet were bare. Her legs, thin and graceful, were tucked beneath her. Her shoulders were narrow and somehow powerful. Her arms and hands were delicate, but I hardly noticed them. I was more interested in the shiny metal object they held.

It was shaped like a long golden stick, with keys to push and a hole at the end. There was another hole on the side, and she blew into it while pressing the keys with her fingers. Notes came out, but they were more than notes. They seemed to dance above her head, swooping and swirling, then fluttering off.

I watched and listened. Jeremy blinked nervously, reminding me of the way people had responded that day in the City when I sang. Like me, Jeremy came from a place where people were afraid of music. I knew they were wrong but wasn't sure why. Music was leading me somewhere. Maybe it was here.

The music stopped. The woman lowered the golden stick and opened her eyes. They were green like grass, like emeralds. Like mine. She was looking right at me.

Did you ever have a perfect moment? I had had one in Between when Sal played and I sang. Now, gazing at the woman, I had another one. The world stopped. It slid to a halt and waited. I didn't move.

A long time after that, I noticed her lips were moving. "Welcome," she was saying.

"Thank you," I replied.

Her gaze moved to Jeremy. She studied him and turned to the others.

"Hello, Sal," she said. "Hello, everyone."

Sal had met her before, and so had his friends. After all my doubts and worries, he had known exactly where he was headed.

"Are you going to show them?" Deb asked her.

"Oh yes," the woman said.

She turned to Jeremy and me. Rising from the rock, she said, "Follow me, both of you."

"Where are we going?" I asked.

She smiled. "To my home."

"We'll stay here and keep watch," Sal told us.

The woman strode off beside the stream, carrying the golden stick. Not knowing what else to do, I followed and Jeremy came along behind me. I tried to imagine the place where she lived—small and cozy, warm and inviting. I thought I would like it.

She hummed as she walked, as naturally as breathing. Her stride was firm. Her body was thin but strong. Her long gray hair swished as she moved. It reminded me of Eleesha's paintbrush.

We were climbing a hill. As we rose, the trees thinned out. The sound of the stream changed from a gurgle to a low roar. The farther we walked, the louder it got. Soon I saw why.

At the top of the hill was a waterfall, tumbling to a pile of boulders beneath. As impressive as it was, I barely noticed.

Beyond the waterfall, surging to the sun, was a stack of silver shapes. They were immense, like game pieces tossed by giants. They had points and edges and smooth sloping sides.

I stopped and stared. The woman turned around and watched me.

"Isn't it wonderful?" she said.

"What is it?" asked Jeremy.

"My home."

"It's more than that," I said. "It's the Music Place."

# PART FOUR

# THE SONG

# 22

## CALLIE

The Music Place rose up before us, spread out across the sky. It looked real, but I had the feeling that if I reached out to touch it, my hand would pass straight through.

The woman led us beside the waterfall and up to the shapes that seemed like a building. I touched one and my hand didn't pass through. The surface was warm. It was solid and shiny. In it, I could see my reflection. My hair was a mess. My clothes were too. Behind me stood Jeremy, staring upward.

The silvery shapes, like Jeremy and me, showed flaws when you got up close. There were dents. Vines and branches had grown over and between.

The woman led us up some steps that were

cleverly hidden among the shapes. We went almost to the top. I looked behind me. Trees stretched as far as I could see.

When I turned back around, a dark figure was blocking my way, silhouetted against the clouds. His shoulders were broad, and his hair stuck out in clumps. His hands grabbed for me.

"Aaugh!" he bellowed.

I stumbled back, nearly falling. Jeremy caught me and turned to the figure. "Who are you?" he demanded.

The woman chuckled. "That's Booker. Don't mind him."

The sun went behind a cloud, and Booker's face emerged. He had dark skin and freckles, with brown eyes that searched me. His arms were still extended, but now they seemed to be reaching out, not grabbing.

The woman said, "I met Booker years ago in Between. He wandered by one day, lost and confused. I liked him, and we became friends. He's been with me ever since. He doesn't talk, but he understands."

The woman reached the top of the steps, gently guided Booker to one side, and gestured to us. "Come in, won't you?"

She opened a door. I moved past Booker, who smiled.

Inside, it was like a different building, a different world. The shapes and reflections were gone. So was the brightness. Instead there was wood—warm, dark, comforting. We were high up in an immense room, like Sal's cave but a hundred times larger, surrounded by seats. In the ceiling was a huge window with light streaming to the floor. Far below us, a platform shone like a jewel.

The woman followed my gaze. "That's the stage," she said. "It's where I play music. The sound is wonderful."

A figure stepped onto the platform. Squinting to see it, I realized it was Booker. I wondered how he had gone so quickly from the steps to the stage.

He clicked his tongue and laughed softly. I heard the sounds clearly, as if he were standing beside me. Then he wandered off, blending into the dark-brown walls.

The woman smiled. "This place is remarkable, isn't it? It's always been this way, like a beautiful instrument."

"What's an instrument?" asked Jeremy. I was

startled to see him standing beside me. For a moment there, it had seemed like just the woman and me.

The woman held up her golden stick. "This is an instrument. I use it to play music. Would you like to hear more?"

* * *

She knelt on the stage, at the center of that vast, empty space, and filled it with music. She breathed into the golden stick, moving the keys, changing the tones, lifting us up to where the light came from. Each note was separate and distinct, and yet they blended together to create long, looping melodies, songs you wanted to chase and explore.

We might have listened five minutes or five hours; I couldn't say which. Then the woman stopped and moved to the edge of the stage, where she sat down and dangled her feet off the side, gazing fondly at us.

"Long ago, before the Warming," she said, "music belonged to the people. They gathered in groups called orchestras, with a hundred members or more, and made music together."

I thought of Deb's story and Pam's drawing of the Music Place. They had made it into a myth, but the woman's words seemed different, like something in the real world.

"Each person played an instrument," the woman continued. "One of the instruments was this one, the flute."

She lifted the golden stick and held it up for us to see. So, it was called a flute. I liked my name better.

"Some instruments were made of wood, such as bassoons, oboes, and clarinets. The trumpets, trombones, French horns, and tubas were made of brass. Some things you would hit, like the drums, tympani, and xylophones. Some, like violins, violas, cellos, and basses, had strings that you plucked and bowed."

Her face lit up when she recited the names, as if they were old friends. Then she looked over at me and cocked her head. "I think you play an instrument."

I thought of my voice. I didn't hit it, pluck it, or blow into it, but it made music. Surely it was an instrument too.

Jeremy studied the woman. "How did you know about the instruments?"

"An old man told me."

"Was he in an orchestra?" asked Jeremy.

She looked at him thoughtfully. "No, but he

carried on their tradition. The orchestras died out during the Warming, and those beautiful musicians dropped away, one by one. Their instruments were lost, except for a few, like this one. The man taught me to play it, as he had been taught, along with others stretching back through time. The orchestras are gone. Now I'm the orchestra."

The woman smiled, then closed her eyes, brought the golden stick to her lips, and blew. The notes formed a picture in my mind, as lovely as anything Eleesha had ever painted.

When she finished, Jeremy said, "Who was the old man? How did you meet him?"

The woman looked past Jeremy to another time and place. "It happened on Freedom Day. I was thirteen years old. That day, my parents let me roam the City. I was exploring an alley and heard something. It was music, the forbidden sound, but it was like nothing I'd ever heard. It seemed to be solid—tall, wide, deep, with every color of the rainbow.

"I followed it and came to an open window. Peering inside, I saw an old man sitting at a table that had a machine on top of it. The machine was a wooden box with a round, flat platform on top and a flared horn sticking up from the back. On the side was a handle, and when the old man cranked it, the platform spun around. There was a plastic disk on the platform, and on top of that was a metal arm with a needle at one end. As the disk spun, music poured from the horn.

"I don't know how long I stood there, listening. The man put on disk after disk, each with a different kind of music. I went inside, and he showed me more disks, which he called records. He had boxes of them. The machine was a phonograph. The sound was an orchestra.

"The man had never heard an orchestra in person, but he had learned to play an instrument. It was the trumpet, a brass horn that he blew to create melodies. When I asked if I could try it, he gave me this flute. From the moment I touched it, it was like part of my body. The old man taught me to play melodies on it."

Jeremy looked at me. I could tell what he was thinking, so I said it for him.

"Music is forbidden. Didn't someone try to stop you? You know, the catchers or…"

"The dreambenders? Oh yes, I know all about

them." She studied Jeremy. "You're one of them, aren't you? But you seem different."

"How do you know about the dreambenders?" he asked.

"That's a different story for a different time. As for your first question, I held on to music by avoiding the catchers and following directions."

"Directions?" I said.

"On the phonograph. Taped to the bottom and handed down through the generations. The directions explained that sometimes, suddenly, we would lose interest in music for a while."

"Dreambenders," said Jeremy.

"That's right, though the early musicians didn't know the word. The directions said that whenever we lost interest, we should keep playing the phonograph, and our love of music would return. And it did, for musician after musician—for the old man and for me."

"He let you play it?"

She nodded. "He had reinforced one of his rooms so it was soundproof. That's where we played the phonograph. It's where he gave me music lessons."

Music lessons. What an idea—that you didn't

just hear music or play it. You worked at it. You studied it to get better.

"That day when you met him," I said, "why wasn't he in the soundproof room? Why was the window open?"

"Freedom Day," said Jeremy.

The woman smiled. "That's right. It was the one day of the year when he risked bringing the phonograph out into the open, one small gesture of defiance."

I looked around at the Music Place, with its warm-brown walls and vaulted ceiling. "How did you get here?"

"Years later, after I'd grown up, the old man realized his health was failing and said he had something to show me. He brought me to the Music Place. The minute I saw it, I knew I had come home.

"When the old man died, he left me the phonograph and records. I brought them to the Music Place. I've lived here ever since."

Jeremy said, "The dreambenders haven't found you? Can't they follow your dreams?"

"We didn't have to," someone said. "We followed you. Or rather, I followed you."

I turned around. There, grinning, was Leif.

# 23

## JEREMY

I gaped at Leif. "How did you find us?"

He flashed a tight grin. "I'm a fixer. That's my job."

"But we were so careful," said Callie.

Leif shrugged. "To me it was obvious where the two of you went. Between would be a good place to hide. So I got a team of fixers and went there."

I said, "That day in the woods, you walked right past us. We were in the trees."

He said, "You think I didn't know? I waited off to the side, and when you came down, I followed you. That's how I got here."

I thought of the girl with the skinny dog. Somehow she had missed him. All of us had. Leif knew about the Music Place, and now so would the dreambenders.

"I'm sorry," I told the woman.

"Who are you?" Leif asked her. "Why are you here?"

"This is my home," she said. "Music is my gift."

*Music.* Leif blanched when he heard the word, but Callie seemed to glow. She was different in this place. She had a warmth, a brightness. It was hard to describe, but it lit up the room.

"Are you a computer?" the woman asked her.

Callie didn't hesitate. "I'm a singer."

The woman smiled. "Of course you are. You have a gift. Everyone does."

"What are you calling a gift?" asked Leif. "What does it even mean?"

"It's what you were born to do," she told him. "Sometimes it takes a while to find it. You watch. You listen. You dig deep to discover it. Then comes the big question: How will you use it? For good? Evil? Safety? Hope?"

I studied her face. She was telling my story, whether she knew it or not.

"What about me?" I asked. "What's my gift?"

"What do you think it is?"

I thought for a moment, then smiled. "Asking."

Leif shifted uncomfortably. I thought of another question.

"What about Leif?" I said. "What's his gift?"

The woman turned toward him, one eyebrow raised. "Do you know what it is?" she asked him.

Leif thought for a moment, then looked around at the wood and the light and the space.

He said, "This is my gift—the Music Place. I'll give it to the fixers."

I said, "That's not what I meant."

"It's all that matters," he said. "Come on. We're leaving. I'm taking you back."

Suddenly, off to one side, the stage door swung open. Sal stepped through, along with Deb, Zack, the tall girl, the one-legged boy, and the girl with the skinny dog.

Relief flooded through me, and I turned to Leif. "Looks like you're outnumbered."

"Maybe not," said Leif.

Behind Sal and his friends, the fixers emerged. Dorothy was with them.

"I'm sorry," she said. "It's over."

Later I learned what had happened. When Leif followed us to the Music Place, he'd contacted the fixers, and one of them had hurried to the Meadow to get Dorothy. I guess I should have been flattered that she had come to arrest me personally.

We spent the night under guard at the Music Place. I wanted to be with Callie, but they put us in separate rooms. Desperate, I spent the night trying to figure out how to escape.

The next morning, Leif came to get us. He released Callie first, then brought her to my room. I shoved him and tried to run. Leif grabbed me effortlessly and, using some trick the fixers had taught him, twisted an arm behind my back.

"Go!" I yelled to Callie.

"I can't," she said.

"Yes, you can! He can't hold both of us."

She said, "It's no use, Jeremy. We have to go back."

Her face seemed different. The light was gone. Something about it was dull and lifeless.

Then I knew. Dorothy had been busy in the dreamscape. I imagined her reaching out and tying off a strand, the way she had taught us.

"No!" I moaned.

"It's fine," Callie said. "I'm a computer."

Her hope was gone, snipped off like a lock of hair. And my hope, what shreds of it were left, withered and died. Sensing my reaction, Leif released my arm. I didn't move. There was nowhere to go.

"Why?" I asked him. "Are you really scared of a song?"

He shook his head. "Don't you ever get tired of questions?"

"What are you going to do, Leif? Tie off our dreams? Brick them over? Then what? How far does it go? What if a dream slips by? What if it spreads?"

He smirked. "Like a disease?"

"Like joy. You can't contain it forever. Somewhere deep inside, it's growing. You can't stop it."

"Watch me," he said.

Callie touched my arm. Her hand was cold. "Thank you for trying. It's better this way."

"What about the Music Place?" I asked her. She gazed at me vacantly.

The fixers came. Dorothy was with them. She took Callie away, back to the City.

Leif turned to me. "Let's go."

"What about the woman who lives here?" I

asked. "What about Sal and the others?"

"Don't you worry about them," he said.

Leif and the fixers led me off. After all the running and dreaming and hoping, I was going back to the Meadow. The Council waited.

# 24

## CALLIE

My mother was sitting by the window, watching. As Dorothy and I approached the house, she came flying through the front door and threw her arms around me.

"You came back! I knew you would!"

"Hi, Mom," I said. It felt warm inside her arms.

My father was right behind her. He hugged us both, his cheek wet against mine.

Dorothy introduced herself and said, "She was in Between."

My father stared at me, amazed. "Between? Weren't you scared?"

"I think so," I said. "It's a little hazy. There was a boy named Jeremy. He talked about dreams."

"He was confused," said Dorothy. "He won't bother you anymore."

I remembered the excitement on Jeremy's face and wondered what had caused it.

My father turned to Dorothy. "Thank you for bringing her back."

Dorothy smiled. "You have a special girl. Take care of her."

That was the end of my big adventure. I went back to my life at home and at the computing center. It was safe and comfortable. Every once in a while, when I was thinking about numbers, an image flashed by with strange faces and bright colors, but then it was gone.

The bright colors reminded me of Eleesha and her friends. I saw them a few days later, when I was on break at the computing center. Eleesha came running up, concerned.

"Well?" she said. "What happened?"

I shrugged. "I decided to come back."

"That's it? What about the boy? You ran away with him."

"Jeremy? He's gone. He went home."

"He talked about a mountain and a path," said

Eleesha. "What was all that?"

"I'm not sure. I don't remember."

She studied my face. "You're different. Like when you stayed away from the Midway. Like we are when we forget our painting and have to remind each other."

"I'm fine," I said.

"What about singing?" she asked. "What about music?"

"We're not supposed to talk about it. You know that."

Eleesha shook her head. "Something isn't right. It shouldn't be this way."

"How should it be?" I asked.

She struggled to speak. "There's something inside you. I want to reach in and pull it out, but I don't know how."

"Numbers," I said. "That's what's inside of me."

* * *

A few days later, as I walked home from work, a woman fell in beside me. She wore a dress that was more like an old sack, but she wasn't dirty. Her skin was soft and smooth. It seemed to shine. There was a bag slung over her shoulder. She was like no one I'd ever seen, and yet there was something familiar about her.

She said, "Hello, Callie."

"Have we met?" I asked.

"Yes. At the Music Place."

I didn't know the place she was talking about, but I knew Jeremy, the boy who had gone with me to Between. For some reason I couldn't recall his face. I did remember his hand and the way it had felt when he touched me.

"Do you know Jeremy?" I asked.

"I do," she told me. "I'd like to see him again."

"He talked about dreams. I remember that."

Once again I tried to picture his face, and part of it came into view. It was his eyes. They were warm and kind.

"He's a different sort of boy," said the woman.

Another part came into view—his nose. I giggled. "Noses are funny."

"Jeremy asks questions," said the woman.

I saw his lips. I had touched them. I had kissed them. I must have blushed, because the woman smiled.

"He's your friend," she said. "He's a dreambender."

I stopped walking. I stood perfectly still, and the world spun around me. The woman watched.

I said, "Dreambender—I know that word. It's important, isn't it?"

"Yes."

"Tell me," I said. "I want to know."

She took my hand. "I'd rather show you."

This time I didn't stop at home. The woman led me to the edge of the City. When no one was looking, we entered Between. My father had said it was frightening, and maybe it was, but it was also familiar.

I remembered another face, this one smudged with dirt.

"Sal," I said. "He had friends. Will we see them?"

"Not this time," said the woman. "We have to hurry."

"Why?"

"Jeremy's in trouble."

"Where is he?" I asked.

"The Meadow."

"On the other side of Between." The phrase popped out of my mouth, as if we were playing a game of fill-in-the-blanks. How did I know that? How many blanks were there?

The woman plunged ahead. I followed, stepping over roots, pushing aside branches.

We walked all that day and the next. I thought of

my parents and how worried they must have been. I thought of my job and imagined the black marks that would be put in my book. These things should have bothered me, but they didn't. I was going to help Jeremy, the boy with the warm eyes and the face I had trouble recalling.

Who was the woman? She knew me, but I didn't know her. She had upset my world, but she made me feel calm and peaceful.

We slept beneath the trees. There was something so simple about it—walk all day, eat roots and berries when we got hungry, sleep at sunset, rise at dawn. We barely talked. We didn't need to. Once or twice I heard sounds behind us and thought we were being followed, but it must have been my imagination.

When I woke up on the third day, the woman was kneeling by a river at the edge of the woods, studying her reflection. She splashed water on her face, then took a brush from her bag and combed her hair. She turned to me.

"This is the day, Callie."

"Are we going to the Meadow?"

"We're there," she said.

# 25

## JEREMY

I tried to feel joy. I really did.

I had asked Leif how he and the dreambenders could contain it, but now, back in the Meadow, it was fading fast. How can there be joy when you're locked in a room and the walls are closing in around you? Joy had faded with Callie's dull stare and Leif's stern glance. The two most important people in my world had changed, and there was nothing I could do about it.

Callie's dream had been erased. Dreambenders had tied it off, and all that was left was rattling around inside my head. That's the way we did things in the Meadow, the place where, until a few days ago, I had lived my life. Then I'd gone to the City. It was noisy and confusing, but it was full of life—real life, flesh-and-blood life, the kind you could touch. I had touched Callie, and she had touched me. Together we had found another place, different from the dreamscape and the City and Between.

The Music Place.

Naming it, hearing the words, I felt a kind of excitement, or the memory of it, the way you remember fire but can't feel the heat.

There was a click, and the door opened. Arthur entered.

"It's time, Jeremy."

I'd been in the room for several days, waiting for the trial. Arthur had brought me food, and I'd tried to talk with him, but he'd just shaken his head sadly. He didn't seem as strong as before, and I guessed that he had been blamed for some of the things I'd done. That made three lives I'd wrecked, if you counted mine, which, it was becoming clear, no one else did.

What's the opposite of a dreambender? Is it a dreamsmasher? A dreamcrusher? When Leif brought me back to the meadow, he had marched me past the dreaming field, and everyone had stared—strangers, friends, Phillip, Anna, Gracie. Gracie had hurt the most. She had joined me in pushing the boundaries, but she had known when to stop. Some of us never learn that lesson. Leif had walked me to a boat and taken me to the island, where I'd been locked in a room until the trial. Now the trial was here.

Arthur led me down a hallway toward the Council chamber. I told him, "I'm sorry, Arthur."

"We're all sorry," he said.

We entered the Council chamber, where once again I faced a long desk with three chairs behind it. Seated in them, as before, were Dorothy, Louisa, and Ching-Li, wearing their dark robes. Leif stood nearby. He gave me a curt nod. He and I had been best friends. I wondered where we had gone wrong.

Louisa said, "Please take your place."

I sat in the chair facing the desk. Leif and Arthur stood on either side of me.

Dorothy pounded a gavel and fixed her gaze on me. "Jeremy, you showed such promise. You were brilliant and intuitive, a natural dreambender who could have been so much more. You asked questions. You pushed us to reconsider things, and that was good. But you pushed too far. You challenged the Plan. You violated the teachings of Carlton Raines, and we can't allow that."

Clearing her throat, Louisa read the charges. "You disobeyed the watchers. You went to the City. You met a dreamer. You told her about the Meadow. You described dreambenders."

As she read each charge, the others flinched as if they'd been struck. When she finished, Ching-Li looked up at me.

"What do you have to say for yourself?" he asked.

Feelings pressed in on me. Hope swirled, then sputtered. I felt as if I weighed a thousand pounds.

Finally I said, "I told Arthur I was sorry. I didn't mean to hurt anyone. But I don't regret what I did. The dreambenders are trying to do the right thing, but it's wrong. The City people should decide for themselves. They need to make mistakes."

Behind me, Leif snorted. "And destroy the world?"

"Or make it better than you could imagine," I said. "One little dream in a forgotten corner of the dreamscape might be the answer to everything. Don't bend it. Let it go. See where it leads."

Dorothy gazed at me. I saw her hesitate.

Then she said, "Jeremy Finn, we find you guilty. You are banned from the dreamscape forever."

She pounded the gavel, and the Council rose. Arthur took my arm. I stood up, barely knowing where I was or what had happened.

As we turned to leave, I heard music.

It was faint at first, then filled the room. It was all around us. There was a melody with straight, pure tones and lovely curved lines. The notes were stacked on top of each other like stones.

"Wait," said Dorothy.

# 26

## JEREMY

There was the strangest expression on Dorothy's face—happiness, regret, longing, all at once. She followed the music out of the Council chamber and into the main room, and the rest of us followed along behind.

In the room, the watchers had been working on the Plan, but they had stopped. They stared just as Dorothy and Arthur and the Council all stared.

Next to the fireplace, playing the golden stick, stood the woman. Callie was beside her.

When Callie saw me, she ran across the room and threw her arms around me. Leif smirked. The others, listening to the music, didn't seem to notice.

"You came," I whispered.

Callie nodded. I saw a spark in her eyes and suddenly knew that no one—not Leif or I or any other dreambender—could put it out for long.

The melody wound around us and between us. Dorothy ventured up to the woman and gazed at her. When the music stopped, the woman lowered the golden stick. Leif moved to intercept her, but Dorothy waved him away.

"I always wanted to meet you," Dorothy told her.

"Really?" asked the woman.

"It was years ago. You dreamed about playing the flute. I was assigned to bend your dreams, and I did. But first I listened. You always played that melody."

"It's mine," said the woman. "I made it up then played it over and over again until it sank deep into my bones. All of us have melodies—at least, that's what I believe. Sometimes I make up melodies for others, to express their gifts."

Callie's eyes lit up, as if she had just remembered something. "I have a melody. I sing it in my dreams."

Ching-Li, standing behind Dorothy, had been getting more and more upset. "Music, musicians—we don't talk of these things."

Dorothy told him, "Just this once, I want to

know more." She turned back to the woman. "I kept your dream. I still listen to it, even today."

Louisa, standing beside Ching-Li, gasped and turned away.

"We all have gifts," said the woman. "Mine is music." She gazed at Dorothy. "What's your gift?"

"She's head of the Council," snapped Leif.

"What else?" asked the woman.

Dorothy was quiet for a few moments. She looked down at her hands, as if noticing them for the first time.

"I used to draw buildings. I imagined them, then drew them with a pencil. I wanted to be an architect. I used to dream about building things in the City. I dreamed about the computing center."

The woman snorted. "The computing center is a box to put people in. They've been in boxes ever since. You're in a box."

Dorothy said, "The boxes work."

"Do they?" asked the woman. "They fit together neatly, but life isn't neat. It's messy."

Next to me, Callie spoke up. "Jeremy and I saw a different kind of building. It wasn't a box. It had strange shapes and shiny surfaces. Inside, it was made of wood."

Dorothy's expression softened. "I'd like to see it sometime."

The woman told her, "You could build something like it, you know. Not in your dreams. In the world."

Dorothy gazed at the woman, then gazed out the window, beyond the trees and bushes.

"It could be in Between," she said.

"This is stupid," said Leif.

Watching him, Callie asked, "Back at the Music Place, you never answered Jeremy's question. What's your gift?"

Leif didn't answer, so I answered for him.

"You could have been a mathematician. You could have worked with numbers."

"You mean, like a computer?" asked Callie.

I shook my head. "Computers fumble in the dirt; Leif could write in the air. He could make patterns, discover order—how things function and fit together."

The woman brought the golden stick to her lips and blew. A different melody came out—intricate as an equation, as strong and flexible as a spiderweb. She had created a melody for Leif.

Lowering the golden stick, she asked him,

"Have ideas ever popped into your head? Numbers? Patterns?"

"All the time," he said. "I wish they would stop."

"Melodies pop into mine," she said. "When I see people, I hear music. The melodies have personalities—like you or Dorothy, like Jeremy or Callie.

Callie said, "Jeremy has a melody? Can you play it?"

The woman smiled, then lifted her golden stick and blew. Notes stabbed the air, probing, posing questions and looking for answers. All the questions I had ever asked and more were there—enough for years, for a lifetime. The melody filled me. I could feel myself smile and relax.

When the woman stopped, I said, "Play Callie's."

The woman nodded to Callie, and Callie sang. Of course, I already knew the melody, because I had heard it before in a dream on a mountain. The melody didn't just describe Callie; it *was* Callie, with all her hopes and possibilities.

Callie finished singing. We sat in silence, pondering what might have been and what still could be. I watched the Council consider their own dreams and the dreams of the City.

"The world can be different," I said. "We can

change. All of us can."

When I was growing up, I had learned a lesson: never forget about Leif. If you did, he would spring up in the most unexpected places—behind a bush, in a crowd, under your bed. He would have that wild, dangerous grin on his face, the way he was grinning now as he came up behind Callie and gripped her neck.

"Don't move," he told us.

# 27

## JEREMY

I moved toward Leif, and he tightened his grip. I watched, helpless, as Callie struggled. Her face was white, her eyes open wide.

Leif's gaze swept the room. "Jeremy's gift is asking. Mine is saying no. You're about to make a mistake, all of you. But I won't let you."

Dorothy said, "Leif, don't do this."

He shook his head. "You've lost your will. I'm in charge now."

Leif's anger was a weapon. I had a weapon too.

"Why?" I asked him.

He snorted. "Don't you ever get tired of questions?"

"What are you going to do, Leif? Hurt Callie? Hurt us all?"

"Maybe," he said. "Maybe not."

"Then what? You think the fixers will back you up? What about the Council? What about Dorothy?"

He glanced at her. "She's weak."

Dorothy watched him, concerned. "Leif, this isn't the way we solve problems. We don't use violence. You know that."

"Jeremy wants change," said Leif. "Maybe violence isn't so bad. Maybe it makes you strong."

"You don't believe that," she told him.

I said, "Think about it, Leif. Can you pull this off? Are you really that good? Are you that smart?"

A drop of sweat ran down his forehead and into his eyes. He wiped it away. His hand was shaking.

"You always were the strongest," I said. "You don't need violence. Maybe you need change. There's strength in that, isn't there?"

I had grown up with Leif. He'd been my best friend. I knew him as well as I knew myself. He wouldn't hurt Callie—or would he?

Squeezing harder, he took a step toward the door.

"Aaugh!"

A strange, primitive cry rang out.

Leif looked around. "What was that?"

A black shape loomed in the doorway. Light streamed in behind and around it.

Leif staggered back. He had a familiar, haunted look on his face. It had been years since I'd seen that look, but I knew it at once. At night in the children's house, he used to have nightmares. He would sweat and squirm and cry out. Sometimes I would go into his dream. The dark figure I saw then was the one bearing down on him today.

The shape advanced. "*Aaugh-ee!*"

It was everything that Leif, in his longing for control and power, had ever feared—mystery, defeat, death, nothingness. He feared those things today, and he had feared them as a child when he would wake up next to me, screaming the word he screamed now.

"Boogey!"

Leif stumbled and lost his balance. Seizing the opportunity, I lunged forward, grabbed Callie, and yanked her from his grasp. As I did, the shape went hurtling past me, rammed into Leif, and lifted him off his feet.

When I looked back, Leif was being held by his greatest fear: Boogey...or was it Booker?

"How did he get here?" asked Callie.

"He must have followed us," said the woman.

Off to one side, I noticed Dorothy staring at Booker.

"Do you know him?" I asked.

"Booker?" she said. "He was the most remarkable dreambender I ever met, the greatest of his generation. I thought I'd never see him again."

I studied Booker. His hands were clenched. His dark brow was furrowed, and his mouth worked silently.

"What happened?" I asked. "How did he get... like this?"

"You mean mute?" said Dorothy. "Wordless? He was born that way. Booker was a strange, brilliant child of dreambenders. He couldn't speak but showed great talent for dreambending. He worked mostly on big dreams.

"Then one day, something awful happened. He came across one of those rare, fragile dreams that are too delicate to bend. He kept trying, and the dream shattered. It went dark."

"I saw one of those," I said, remembering the dream that gave off green fog. "What was it? How can a dream go dark?"

Dorothy shook her head sadly. "Once in a great while, as in delicate surgery, a dream is destroyed and the dreamer is damaged. It always seems to be a teenager, at that sensitive age when children become adults."

"Damaged?" I asked. "How?"

"They lose their ability to dream. Worse than that, they lose their memories—sometimes part, sometimes all. They don't know who they are. They wander through the City. When that happens, dreambenders hurry to get them and take them to Between, where they're trained to survive and live out their lives."

"That's terrible," I said. "We're supposed to help people, not hurt them."

Dorothy shook her head sadly. I could see pain in her expression, along with something else that surprised me. It was shame.

"That's what happened to Sal and his friends, isn't it?" I said.

Dorothy nodded. "Remember when I told you I

went to the City on a special assignment? It was to get Sal."

I thought about Sal's description of Binders and suddenly knew where it had come from.

Callie said, "That's so sad."

"Yes, it is," said Dorothy. "When that kind of damage occurs, it's awful—not just for the dreamer but for the dreambender too. In Booker's case, when he realized what he had done he let out a loud bellow, like the one we just heard. He paced the Meadow, overcome with grief. Then one day, he was gone. He just disappeared. We sent out search parties, but they never found him. We tried to track him through his dreams, but there weren't any. It was as if he had dropped off the earth.

"Finally we gave up. I always thought he had wandered away and died, maybe killed himself. Legends grew up around him. The children called him Boogey."

Booker grunted and released Leif. Strong, proud, independent Leif stood there quivering, unable to stop staring at his nightmare.

Dorothy approached Booker and placed her hand on his arm. "Are you all right? Do you understand?"

Booker hesitated, then nodded.

The woman took a cloth from her bag and wiped his forehead. "I was picking berries in Between one day, and Booker came to me, distraught, clearly needing help. I took him home to the Music Place, and he lived there with me. He didn't talk. For a while I thought he didn't dream. Then one night I learned differently.

"I fell asleep and had a vivid, detailed dream. It was pictures, all pictures. No one spoke. They didn't have to. It was Booker, telling his story without words. He showed me the Meadow, the dreambenders, his terrible accident, his escape to Between."

"That can't be right," Dorothy told her. "We adjust dreams. We don't create them."

"Booker does."

"Why didn't we see his dreams or yours?" asked Dorothy. "We would have found out about the Music Place."

"He didn't just create dreams," said the woman. "He learned how to cloak them. He hid his own dreams and mine, so you wouldn't find the Music Place."

Dorothy gazed at him in wonder. Booker, the greatest of his generation, had done things no dreambender had ever done—maybe the kinds of things Dorothy and the watchers had hoped I would do.

Callie said, "Does Booker live with you?"

"Yes," the woman replied. "I think he finds the Music Place comforting. Every once in a while, though, he lets out that cry."

Leif caught my eye. His voice was low and flat. "You're a fool, Jeremy. You ruined everything."

I shot him a sad smile. "We couldn't stop you. But your dreams did."

Turning to Dorothy, I asked, "What happens next?"

"I thought I knew," she said. "Now I'm not sure."

"Maybe that's all right," I said.

# 28

## CALLIE

We walked outside, and the watchers followed. Booker walked with Leif. The breeze blew, carrying the scent of roses. Waves lapped against the shore. The sun was brilliant, not yellow but a pure, pure white.

The woman looked out over the water, then turned to me. "I'm old. You're young. You have the gift."

"The gift?"

"Music," she said. "You create melodies. The melodies live. You can sing the world. I can show you how."

Her gaze was so intense that I had to look away.

"She's a computer," said Ching-Li.

The woman smiled. "Break out of the box.

Build, don't bend. Leave people to their dreams. Let Callie sing."

I thought about the gift—the weight of it, the joy. I could sing every day. I could make music with the woman. I could spin melodies while Eleesha and her friends painted.

Jeremy had asked what would happen next. The answer, it turned out, was simple. The woman closed her eyes, then lifted the stick to her lips and played. I joined in, because I couldn't help it.

The music drifted over the water, toward the land of Between, which didn't seem as wild as before. Seeing the trees, I thought of Sal and the expression on his face when he played the sound box.

When we finished, Jeremy asked me, "Is anything wrong?"

"No," I said. "I just need to do something."

* * *

"Will you just tell me?" said Eleesha, laughing. "Does it have to be a surprise?"

I had found her in the City, painting a building. Leaving Jeremy behind, I had brought her to Between, where I knew Sal would find us. When we arrived, he stepped out from behind a tree.

"Hello," he said.

Eleesha stopped short. She stared at him, her eyes open wide. Then, grinning, she went running and threw her arms around him.

"Sal!"

"Who are you?" he asked.

Eleesha stepped back, startled. She looked at me.

"I'm sorry," I told her, "but I realized that when he plays music, he has the same expression you do when you paint. I had to bring you here to see if it was him, but I didn't want to get your hopes up. So it had to be a surprise."

"Why doesn't he recognize me?" asked Eleesha.

"I'll tell you," I said, "but first, can we get something to eat? I'm starved."

Sal took us to the cave, where he gave us roots and berries. We settled on the ground, and Eleesha glanced around as we ate. She seemed nervous, the way City people get when they're in Between.

I asked her, "You like stories, right?"

She nodded.

"This one is about the Warming," I said.

"What's that?" asked Sal.

Eleesha gazed at him in wonder.

I told him, "The Warming was a terrible time. Rain flooded everything. A few lucky people escaped and lived on a boat for years. When the waters receded, they came to the City. A few of them who had special abilities settled in a place called the Meadow and came to be known as Dreambenders."

"Binders?" said Sal.

"That's right."

"Could I meet one?"

I smiled. "You already have."

Turning back to Eleesha, I went on. "Some of the people studied history and worshiped cemeteries. They lived in the past."

"That's us, isn't it?" said Eleesha. "The City people."

I nodded. "But the dreambenders were different. They controlled the future, by adjusting people's dreams. Sometimes, though, they made mistakes and the dreamers were changed. They stopped dreaming. They lost their memories. When that happened, the dreambenders brought them to Between. Stripped of the past, blind to the future, they lived in the present—eating, sleeping, hunting, playing music."

Sal seemed troubled. "You're talking about me, aren't you?"

Eleesha reached out and took his hand. "You're my brother. I'm your sister, Eleesha. We're twins."

"Twins?" he said.

She smiled. "I've missed you. I go to a bench in the cemetery to think of you."

"What's a cemetery?" he asked.

"I'll show you," said Eleesha. "I can take you home."

He glanced at me, worried. "This is my home."

I told Eleesha, "He's right, you know. He's different now. This is where he lives."

"I like it here," he said.

"Did you bring it?" I asked Eleesha.

She reached inside her jacket, took out a small painting, and handed it to Sal. He gazed at it in wonder. "Did you make this?"

Eleesha nodded. "Do you like it?"

Sal didn't answer. Instead, he went into the cave and brought out the sound box. Sitting next to Eleesha, he gazed at the painting and played its colors—green, red, a deep blue.

When he finished, Eleesha said, "This is your home. Can I come visit? We could be friends."

* * *

That was when the world changed.

Things are different now. The dreambenders, after years of hiding, showed themselves to the people of the City. At first the people were angry, hardly able to believe what the dreambenders had done. Gradually, though, they came to understand that the dreambenders, misguided though they had been, were trying to help. In the end, it may have been music that saved us.

The woman showed the people her golden stick. Sal played his sound box. I sang. The people listened, frightened at first but growing to like it. Some sang along. A few disappeared into their homes and brought out instruments, keepsakes that had been passed down and hidden away. The people tried to play them, and a new orchestra was born.

The dreambenders, hesitant at first, opened the Meadow and invited people in. Jeremy's friends led the way. Gracie gave tours. Hannah served food. Phillip explained dreambender philosophy.

The City dwellers were amazed—first, that such a place existed, hidden away in a far corner; and second, that it was so simple and small. Their dreams and lives had been controlled by just a handful of people, sitting in a field under the stars.

And the dreambenders? They were out of a job. But with the help of Dorothy and Arthur and the woman, they adjusted. There was talk of lessening the pain they had caused by partnering with dreamers to help and heal. We're not sure yet how this will work, but we have faith that it will.

Jeremy and I see a lot of each other these days. I visit him in the Meadow, and he comes to the City. Sometimes we take a walk and talk about the way it will be.

When we go to Between, we often see Dorothy. She's building things—a house, a gathering place, an oddly shaped structure that seems to be her favorite. She got rid of her bun and is letting her hair flow down over her shoulders.

The dreambenders aren't the only ones who have needed to change. For City people, the old world was built on assigned roles that were rigid and inflexible. What will the world be like if we can pick a role and then, if it doesn't fit, slip into another one? The people are excited to know, but they are also nervous.

No one, in the City or the Meadow, has all the answers. We do have questions. If we run out,

Jeremy gives us more. We aren't always happy, but we are free. Each year, we celebrate it on Freedom Day—not freedom from, as Pam and Juanita remind us, but freedom to.

We are free to roam. The City people, no longer bound by fear, explore Between and come to the Meadow. Dreambenders visit the City.

Sal and his friends roam too, but they prefer their cave and the music Sal creates on his sound box. Sometimes Eleesha stays with him in the cave. In the evenings, he plays. She paints. Deb tells stories. The tall girl sits back, listening and watching. These days, Sal isn't afraid of Binders. He knows they're people like him, trying to do what's best.

In the Meadow, on the island, there used to be a sign on the wall.

> Never meet the dreamer.
> Never harm the dreamer.
> Always follow the Plan.

Arthur took down that sign and put up another one.

Created in song.
Explored in dreams.
Discovered in life.

It's not always clear what we should do, but Jeremy tells us that's the way it's supposed to be. People must decide for themselves. There is danger because they can be hurt. The Earth can be damaged, as it was in the Warming, and everything might be destroyed. But we need freedom, because if we can't fall, we can never fly.

Now that things are changing, the City people dream of the future. Dreambenders explore the past. Sal and his friends are showing us how to live the moments in between.

I go to the Music Place. The woman is there, and so is Booker. I'm learning about songs and how to sing them. Even Jeremy has tried playing music. He found the old man's trumpet and blew a few notes, then decided to stick with his questions.

Recently, Jeremy has been spending time with an old friend. He and Leif go to the dreaming field, where they sit and talk. Sometimes they argue, the way they've always done. Sometimes they actually listen. I think Jeremy is helping Leif, but Jeremy says it helps both of them. Leif is teaching Jeremy about discipline and control. Every once in a while, Leif asks a question.

Leif is learning as he goes. So is Jeremy. Maybe all of us are. We are hummed into life. The hum becomes a melody, the melody a path, the path a journey.

We are singers, living the song.